Outback Hope:
The Farmer

ANNIE SEATON

The Augathella Girls: Book 8

ISBN 978-0-6457010-2-9

THE AUGATHELLA GIRLS

Book 1: Outback Roads –The Nanny
Book 2: Outback Sky – The Pilot
Book 3: Outback Escape – The Sister
Book 4: Outback Winds – The Jillaroo
Book 5: Outback Dawn – The Visitor
Book 6: Outback Moonlight – The Rogue
Book 7: Outback Dust – The Drifter
Book 8: Outback Hope – The Farmer

Coming in 2023: a series of short and sweet stories
about the Augathella crew. Catch up with old
friends, and meet some new characters in:
An Augathella Easter
An Augathella Baby
An Augathella Surprise
An Augathella Wedding
An Augathella Winter
An Augathella Ball
An Augathella Spring
An Augathella Christmas

Augathella Characters - Book 8

Kimberley Riordan	Deputy Principal
Quinn Calthorpe	*Merry Downs Station*
Braden and Callie	*Kilcoy Station*
Kent and Sophie Mason	*Lara Waters*
Jacinta and Ryan Francesco	Former residents
Harry Higgins and Laura Adnum	Local doctor & midwife
Rory, Nigel and Petie	Braden's sons
Jon and Fallon Ingram	Station managers
Ben Riley and Amelia Foley	Shire engineer & station hand
Matt Randall and Bec Hunter	Accountant and nurse
Old Reg	Local character
Bob Hamblin	School Principal
Beth Riordan	Kimberley's sister
Claudia Ricci	Casual school teacher

Prologue

Kimberley

Kimberley and Jacinta waited near the bar at the Augathella pub until there was a gap in the crowd. The place was buzzing; it was very different to the usual quiet Sunday afternoon.

'It's the biggest crowd I've seen here since the weekend Ryder showed up with his dance troupe. That was a night and a half, wasn't it?' Kimberley chuckled.

Jacinta nodded. 'I didn't think so when I saw him walk in. I really thought Ryder was a stripper! But it ended well.' She looked down at the engagement ring on her left hand.

'What made me smile was the embarrassed faces at school drop off the next week,' Kimberley said. 'Some of those school mums knew how to party that night.'

Braden and Callie had called their friends to come in for lunch at the Augathella pub. They'd taken a couple of days to travel back from Brisbane, and had decided to have lunch before they did the grocery shopping and went out to *Kilcoy Station*. The word that the Cartwrights were back had spread around town, and it seemed as though half the population had arrived. The two girls stepped forward as two men left the bar. They squeezed in close to the end of the counter and waited their turn to be served.

'We'll miss you when you move to Brisbane, Jacinta,' Kimberley said as they waited.

'I hope you can pick up someone to replace me fairly quickly. Otherwise, it's going to be tight staff-wise.' Even though she was looking forward to a new start with Ryder in Brisbane, and a new school, she'd be sad to leave her hometown, and the small school and the teachers and kids that made up her work community.

'Term four's not too bad with all the Christmas activities and end-of-year stuff. We'll be fine.' Kimberley grinned. 'And we've always got Claudia on call.'

Jacinta rolled her eyes. 'Beggars can't be choosers. I'm sorry I have to go so soon, but Ryder's old boss wants him to start straight away, and I didn't want him to leave without me.'

'True love,' Kimberley nudged her and grinned.

'I'm happy.' Jacinta smiled and Kimberley sent a glance to the corner of the bar behind Jacinta as Quinn Calthorpe's deep voice filled the sudden lull in the conversations around them. When they'd walked into the bar, Kimberley had noticed him sitting there, nursing a beer, looking unhappy, but she'd turned away.

They had nothing in common now. Forget any past history; that was the safest way.

Jacinta followed her gaze. 'Quinn Calthorpe's not looking very happy these days. Weren't you pair an item once?'

Kimberly felt the heat rise in her cheeks. 'No, never an item. Just good mates. He was friends with my sister, Beth, at school, and part of the gang that spent a lot of time at our place when we were growing up.'

'I keep forgetting you're local too,' Jacinta said. 'You were a few years behind me at school.'

Kimberley smiled. 'I'm not that much younger.'

'No, you're not.' Jacinta laughed and nudged her with an elbow. 'About time you got yourself a fella, honey. Romance seems to be in the Augathella air lately.'

'Just because you're engaged, doesn't mean I have to go down that track.' Heat rose in Kimberley's face. 'I'm a career woman through and through. I'm aiming for Bob's job when he retires next year.'

'And you'd be the perfect person for it. Ah, here comes Bill now. So, bubbles for you or a wine?'

'I'll just have a soft drink, thanks. I'm going to school after lunch is over.' Kimberley had bought the last round of drinks and she'd only come over to the bar to help Jacinta carry the trays of drinks to the table. Coming over had nothing to do with Quinn being propped up at the end of the counter.

She took a step back as Jacinta gave the order to Bill, the long-time barman.

As the pub noise increased in volume, Kimberley could still hear the low tones of Quinn's voice. She'd always loved his voice. A deep timbre and he rounded his words slowly. But now he sounded miserable as he spoke into his phone. He was staring down into his beer, his face creased in a frown as he pressed the mobile to his ear.

It was out of character for Quinn to be like that. He'd always been the life and soul of the gang as they'd grown up. Once her sister and friends had left town and gone off to uni and work, she and Quinn had become close friends. They'd lost touch when Quinn had moved away a few years before his mum died.

'Off to get more experience in the Territory so he can eventually take over when his father is ready,' Beth had told her. It had hurt Kimberley that Beth and Quinn seemed to stay in touch.

Then Quinn's dad passed away earlier this year, and Quinn had come home a few weeks ago to take over the station. Kimberley hadn't seen him since he'd come back to town, but now, looking at him, she noticed how much weight he'd lost. These days, he had a rugged, wiry look about him. His face was gaunt, and she hadn't seen him smile since she'd come into the pub.

Not that she'd looked over his way that much.

Okay, maybe a couple of times. They'd been good mates back in the day, even though she was a couple of years younger than him.

Quinn had been a strong and strapping teenager, skilled in cattle work, and he'd always won the bull riding events at the annual rodeo in town. Kim had loved watching him ride but she hadn't been to a rodeo for years. There was always something to do at school on the weekends and she didn't set aside much time for socialising.

For a while back when she was in year ten, Kim had thought that her sister and Quinn might end up together, but when she'd asked Beth before she went off to uni, her sister had laughed.

'Me and Quinn? He's my buddy. No romance there, Kimmy.'

Sixteen-year-old Kim had filed that away with a little bit of hope. She shook her head; where had the years gone? She was closer to thirty than twenty now and those dreams of her youth had turned to dust. Quinn had moved away, and she went off to uni and had barely given him a thought until she'd heard his mum was ill.

Merry Downs was one of the showpiece

stations in the region. Kim always remembered the one time she'd been allowed to tag along with Beth and the group to an afternoon pool party out there when she'd been about fifteen. As she waited for their drinks, her thoughts went back to the night she met Quinn Calthorpe.

Chapter 1

Kimmy

Kim's older sister, Beth, and her group had just left school and were about to head off to the big smoke for uni and jobs, and the Calthorpes had held a farewell party for the group of kids who were leaving town.

Kim knew Quinn from school as one of the seniors, but being invited along to the party with Beth had made her feel pretty grown-up. She still remembered what she wore that night. A pair of denim shorts and a halter neck top in a pretty pale pink and lemon check, tied in a knot around her waist. The shirt was probably still somewhere in the back of a drawer; even though she was still the same size she was way too old to wear stuff like that these days. She must have looked okay that afternoon because she'd noticed some of the guys checking her out.

Beth came over while the barbeque was cooking in the breezeway and gave her a raspberry vodka Cruiser. 'One drink, Kimmy. That'll do you, but don't tell Mum or she'll kill me.'

Kimberley had sat back and watched the hilarity as Beth and her friends jumped into the pool. The boys showed off with high dives from the high rock wall at the end, and when the girls got out of the water, they lay around on the grass in their bikinis. Kim didn't feel confident enough to put her bikini on, and she also didn't feel comfortable going over to sit with the older girls. They were Beth's friends; she was quite happy to be on the fringe and watch the fun.

A loud yell caught her attention. 'Don't you go any higher, Julia.' Braden Cartwright was climbing up the rock wall to where his girlfriend, Julia, sat on the highest rock. They'd been a couple since they were fifteen. Kim hadn't been interested in boys; all the boys in her year were so immature.

'Hey, Kimmy. Are you having a good time?'

She jumped as a deep voice spoke close to her ear—the music volume had been ramped up. Turning around, Kim was surprised to see Quinn Calthorpe sitting on the grass beside her holding a can of Coke.

'I am,' she said. 'Thank you for letting me come this afternoon.'

'Are you supposed to be drinking?' He gestured to the bottle she was holding.

'I'm allowed to have one. Beth gave it to me.'

'Well, if you see Mum or Dad come out, get rid of it. They are absolute sticklers about underage drinking. Mum'll do the rounds shortly.'

'Okay, I wasn't enjoying it anyway.' Kim

12

tipped the bottle over and emptied it out on the lawn.

'You didn't have to do that,' Quinn said.

'No, I didn't like it. I could feel it going straight to my head.'

'I'll have to have a word with your big sister. She shouldn't have given it to you. How old are you, Kimmy?

Kim sat up straight, lifted her chin and put her shoulders back. 'I'm almost sixteen.'

He looked surprised. 'Are you? Year ten?'

'Yes, I go into year eleven after Christmas.'

Quinn had sat there beside her for ages, and they chatted about what subjects she was picking up in year eleven and what he was going to do now that he'd finished school.

Kim wasn't surprised to hear that he was going to stay out on the property and help his dad for a year or so.

'And then maybe I'll go off and do some sort of study. Not that I'm keen,' he said. 'I think I'd learn more on the property working with Dad than any uni course. I love this place.'

'It's really beautiful,' Kim said looking around the pool area. 'It's hard to believe we're at the end of a red dirt road in the middle of the outback. Your lawn is so green and lush.' She felt her cheeks heat. 'When we first drove in, I thought it was that artificial turf. Even in town, our grass is dry and brown. I've never seen such a lovely house and pool or felt grass as soft as this.' She ran her fingers over the soft broad-leafed grass. 'You wouldn't credit it way out here. It's like paradise.'

'That's the advantage of being on top of the Great Artesian Basin,' he said. 'We're pretty lucky out here. Dad's grandfather chose this land because of all the springs. We even have some hot springs.'

'Oh wow, I'd love to see them.' Kim's face heated again. She had to remember that this was probably the only time she'd be here. He wouldn't be interested in taking her out there.

'Do you live in town?' he asked. 'I've never asked Beth, but I picked that up when you said about your grass being dry. Or are you on the land?'

'No, we live in town. Our older sister's already gone to uni. I'm the baby of the family.'

'And have you always lived in Augathella?' He seemed genuinely interested and a warm feeling rushed through Kim. She was feeling very grown up. Quinn was treating her like an adult.

As she recalled that afternoon, she realised it was the first time that she had felt she was growing up. She'd left the silliness of school behind, and she was starting to look forward to what she wanted to do with her life.

Having the interest of a nice-looking guy like

Quinn was a great confidence booster.

'No, we moved here when I was in early primary school.'

'Where from?

'We were out at Quilpie. Dad was working in the stock and station agency there, but he got a job on the council here. He drives down to Charleville every day, but he didn't want to live in Charleville. He said it was too big a town for him.' She rolled her eyes. 'Too big!'

'Do you like living in Augathella?' Quinn asked. He'd rolled over and was stretched out on his stomach on the grass quite close to her.

Kim nodded. 'I do; it's got everything that I want. I enjoy school. I've got good friends and I like watching movies. Sometimes we go down to Charleville for an afternoon or a weekend away. But I'm just as happy at home.'

'Unusual to hear someone satisfied living here,' he commented. 'Most of the girls,' he gestured to the group lying on the lawn on the other side of the pool, 'can't wait to get out and move to the big smoke.'

'Including Beth,' Kim chipped in. 'Will you miss her?' She looked at him from beneath her lashes.

'It'll be a change with all this lot moving away.' He grinned at her. 'But like you, Augathella and the district have everything I want. I'm going to help Dad turn our station into the most successful in the region.'

'Big plans,' she said.

'What about you?' he asked.

Kim rolled over onto her stomach and propped her chin in her hands. Their elbows were also touching, but she felt comfortable close to Quinn.

'I'll probably go off to university,' she said, 'but I'll come back here. I'm going to be a teacher.'

'High school or state?'

Before Kim could answer Beth sauntered over in her minuscule red bikini. Kim was aware of Quinn checking her sister out. A shaft of regret lodged in her chest. Looked like the chummy afternoon was over.

'Did you finish your drink, Kimmy?' she asked.

Kim nodded and didn't let on she'd tipped it out.

'Come in for a swim, Quinn. The water's great.'

Beth reached out to his hands to pull him up and grinned at Kim. 'You too, Kim. Did you bring your togs?'

'No, I didn't. I'm happy here. You two go and swim.'

'Come and sit on the side and dangle your feet in the water,' Quinn said. He reached down once he was on his feet and held out his hand to Kim.

Beth looked at them both with a frown.

Kim followed them over to the pool and sat on the side.

A friendship had been born that afternoon.

Her friendship with Quinn Calthorpe developed over the next two years. Beth and her friends went off to university, and whenever Quinn was coming to town, he'd always send Kim a text and they'd meet at the coffee shop for a milkshake.

Thoughts and dreams were shared, and many a problem was discussed over two chocolate milkshakes.

The day that she'd got her offer for entry into a teaching degree at Griffith University in Brisbane, Quinn had hugged her, but it had been in friendship. Beth told her it was because she was a townie.

'Quinn's mother is a snob, Kimmy,' her sister said. 'He'll have to marry someone on the land. Did you see the airstrip on the property? Most of their entertaining is with Vera's Sydney friends. If she can't get a wealthy landowner's daughter, it'll be a socialite from Sydney for Quinn, so don't get your hopes up.'

Kim shook her head. 'I don't have any hopes. Quinn and I are just really good mates. It doesn't have to be about romance and sex.'

But in her heart, Kim wasn't sure what her feelings were. She was too young to settle down with any guy, and anyway, as much as she yearned for it, Quinn had never ever shown any romantic interest in her.

Until the night before she left for university.

Kimberley, deputy principal of Augathella State School, closed her eyes and pushed away the memory of that night.

Chapter 2

Kimberley

Kimberley's reminiscing was interrupted by Quinn's voice, loud enough now to hear all his words.

'Mate, I can't take any more,' he said. 'It's over. I'm done. I can't put any more energy into it. This is it.'

Quinn frowned as Kimberley glanced across at him, but it wasn't directed at her. The person at the other end obviously tried to talk to him. She turned slowly, trying not to intrude on his private conversation, but the despair on Quinn's face as he pressed the phone to his ear stunned her.

'No mate, you're not going to change my mind. I'm checking out.'

Kimberley froze at his words.

Checking out. What the hell did he mean by that? Surely not what it sounded like?

Jacinta called over her shoulder. 'Here we go, Kim.'

Kimberley slid a sidelong glance at Quinn as she reached for the drink tray.

His head was down and as he stared into his beer he looked totally dejected.

Checking out?

Kimberley decided to forgo her visit to the school this afternoon and catch up with Quinn Calthorpe. Any feelings she'd once had were long gone, but if he thought he was *checking out*, it wouldn't be on her watch.

Kimberly knew him so well. She was the only person who would understand why she was so worried about him. No one else would have an inkling of why she felt that way, and it was even hard to admit to herself that it was from the memory of one night more than ten years ago. The night that she'd hugged to herself for years. His words that night had made it hard for any guy to measure up to Quinn Calthorpe.

She'd had a few relationships at uni, and made some good friends, but nothing had ever pierced the protective shell that had grown around her heart.

But no matter how much she wanted to stay away from Quinn, the words she'd heard terrified her. Kim was determined to help him.

No matter how rude he was to her. He was a grown man now. A man she didn't know, a man very different to the nineteen-year-old guy she'd fallen for all those years ago.

Or that she thought she'd fallen for.

First love was a very different thing from true love. If it had been true love, no matter what Quinn had said, he wouldn't have left her behind.

Chapter 3

Quinn

'Mate, I'm checking out. I've had enough.' Quinn noticed a figure working purposefully over to the bar.

Braden Cartwright. The last person he wanted to see. Someone from his past here.

'Gotta go, Mike. And no, you're not going to change my mind. I mean it. I'm checking out. There's no point.' Quinn disconnected the call to his mate in Darwin and turned to Braden who was standing a little way along the bar. If Quinn had known Braden and many of his high school friends were going to be in the pub this afternoon he wouldn't have come into town. It had been a stupid idea anyway. He'd had three beers so was going to have to hang around a while before he drove back home.

'Quinn. Good to see you, mate.' Braden walked along the bar and stood beside him. 'It's been a long time.'

He and Braden had been great mates at school, and his mother had approved of that friendship. Braden's family had been in the region as long as the Calthorpes. They'd not been far behind the Brassingtons who'd left Roma in 1864 and set up a store on the crossroads on the banks of the Warrego River just after the great flood. The Cartwrights and the Calthorpes had been early settlers in the opening up of the Maranoa and Warrego districts.

Braden held out his hand and Quinn shook it. 'Hey Quinn, great to see you. I haven't seen you for ages. I was going to give you a call this week and come out and see how things were going, now that life's back to normal. You've been back a while now.'

Quinn shook his head. 'No need to come out, mate.' The last thing he wanted was anyone turning up at the station. He had too much to get his head around and didn't need anyone's shock or sympathy interfering with that. 'Sounds like you've had some torrid times.' Quinn knew he had to put things in perspective. He put his hand on Braden's shoulder. 'I was very sorry to hear about Julia.'

'Thanks, Quinn. I had a tough couple of years, but life goes on. You don't realise how good things are when they're normal until something like that happens in one split second. Make sure you value what you've got.'

'True.' Quinn nodded.

'You'll have to meet Callie, my wife, and my boys. Come and join us for lunch. It's a bit of a celebration today. We're just back from Brisbane. We came close to losing our Petie. It was a wake-up call for me. You'd think I would have learned when I lost Julia. It's family that matters. Nothing else. Money doesn't matter, land doesn't matter; it's family and people that're important. Anyway, you just remember that. I'll be in touch.'

'Thanks for the lunch offer, Braden, but I have to get going. I'll meet Callie another day. I heard about your young boy. I'm pleased he's recovered. Reg filled me in when I arrived.'

'Good old Reg, what would we do without him? Can I buy you a beer, Quinn?'

'Nah. Thanks, mate. I've had enough. Gotta drive home, but thanks.' Quinn looked around as he reached into his pocket for his keys. Kim and Jacinta had left the bar, and relief settled in. He didn't need to talk to Kimberley Riordan. It had worried him enough that she'd been in hearing range when he'd been talking to Mike.

'Listen, mate, one of the things I wanted to talk to you about was the meeting in Charleville on Thursday at the town hall. Have you heard about it?'

'No. What meeting?'

'Well, you know how we've all been forced to reduce our breeding herds since that deforestation legislation was passed in 2018?'

Quinn shook his head. 'Queensland legislation?

'Yeah.'

'No, mate. I've been immersed in the industry up in the Territory. I haven't kept up to speed with local stuff over the past few years, and to be honest, Dad wasn't very communicative in his last years. I'm wearing it now though.'

'Problems?' Braden looked at him, concern etched into his face.

Quinn shrugged. 'We'll catch up one day and I'll fill you in when I decide what to do. Is this about making carbon farming look good?'

'That's my view. Overregulation. The bottom line is it makes it bloody hard for us. We're the ones on the ground dealing with drought.'

'Bloody politicians,' Quinn said.

'Yep. The new legislation means more red tape for us trying to feed our stock during drought, and not only that, but we have to find the right balance of trees and grass on our stations.'

'So, what's the meeting about?'

'We know we have to wear it; the legislation's been passed. It's a think tank to get some strategies in place. You should come. Your experience in the Territory will give a fresh perspective.'

'Thursday, you said?' Quinn asked.

'Yeah, five o'clock at the town hall. I didn't know if we'd be back in time, but I'm pleased we are. Things can get back to normal a bit now. Do you know Jon Ingram? He probably wasn't around when you moved away.'

'No, he wasn't, but I know him from up north. We worked together at Cape Crawford.'

'Jon managed my place for a while after Julia passed. Now he's married and settled here, and with a little boy. When we were in Brisbane, I heard he's made an offer on a place out near *Merry Downs*.'

'Sounds like he's settled permanently.'

'Seems so. He's a top bloke. His wife, Fallon, is a helicopter pilot. She was up in the Territory too.'

'Okay. I'll come to the meeting.' Quinn figured he had nothing to lose. You never know, there might be a solution down there. When cattlemen got together, it was amazing what could be shared.

'Great. There are quite a few things I want to talk about since we've had the rain and prices have gone back up. A lot of us are doing pretty well. But I've heard about some steers going cheap if you want to increase your stock levels.'

Quinn swallowed. 'I was just on the phone to my accountant in Darwin.'

'On a Sunday?' Braden raised his eyebrows.

'Yeah, on a Sunday. He's hassling me.'

'To do what?' Braden asked, and then he shook his head. 'I'm sorry. It's not my business, but if you need an ear or advice, don't hesitate.'

'I'll take you up on that.' Quinn looked to the left as Kimberly went back to the bar and collected another tray. As she walked past them, she gave him a quick smile, and he nodded briefly.

The less he saw of Kim Riordan, the better. Quinn knew he had enough problems without throwing guilt into the mix. He didn't have time—or the desire—to think about that at the moment.

'Do you want a lift down on Thursday?'

Quinn nodded. 'Sounds good. How about I meet you here in town?' It would mean saving a tank of fuel going down and back. The new Landcruiser Dad bought was an absolute gas guzzler. He would've sold it, but there was more owing on it than it would sell for. 'I'll give you my number. Give me a buzz Wednesday and let me know what time.'

'Good. I'll pick you up about four. Are you sure you won't join us for lunch?'

'Thanks, but no. Places to go, people to see.'

Huh, Quinn thought. *If only.*

'Okay,' Braden said. 'I'll see you in town on Thursday. And remember, I'm a ready ear if you need to talk. I'll give you my mobile in case there's any change in plans. What's your number?'

Once they'd exchanged numbers, Braden shook his hand again.

'Great to catch up, Quinn. It's been a long time since we hung out together. I'll never forget that pool of yours.'

'We had some good times.'

'And we'll have more now that you're back.'

Quinn picked up his keys as Braden walked away.

'Another one for the road, mate?' the barman asked.

Quinn shook his head. 'No thanks, mate, I'm driving.'

'Have a good day.'

Quinn headed for the door, patting his pocket to make sure his wallet and phone were still there. The buzz of conversation and laughter coming from the bistro was loud. He flicked a glance inside as he walked past the door and his eyes settled on Kim who was talking animatedly to a man he didn't recognise.

He hadn't heard from Kim or Beth since he'd moved away. She'd always been a good friend to him. It was a shame their friendship had taken a dive the night before he'd left town. Quinn had spent way too much time thinking about her since he'd come back to town. He'd read in the local paper that she worked at the state school, so she'd achieved what she'd always wanted. She was probably married with a couple of kids.

Quinn put his head down and walked outside. Old Reg was sitting in his usual position.

'Leaving already, mate? You've only just got

here. You've been gone for long enough. Are you back home for good? Haven't seen you about much since you came back from the north.'

'I don't get to town much, Reg,' he said.

'Sorry to hear about your dad.' Reg lifted up his schooner glass. 'We're all getting on. I suppose I'll be joining him in the not-too-distant future.'

Quinn grinned at him. 'Thanks, Reg. But I disagree. You'll be sitting here in another twenty years, mate. The pub wouldn't survive without you here keeping us all up-to-date with what's going on.'

The wrinkled face cracked into a wide smile. 'Do you know how old I am?'

'I don't, but it's been a topic of conversation at the bar for as long as I can recall.'

'Well, that should give you a clue then.' Reg tapped the side of his nose. 'I had ten years on your dad. I'll be eighty-nine at Easter.'

'You're going well. Sharp as a tack and you don't miss a trick.'

'Someone has to keep an eye on what goes on in town. Speaking of which, what's going on with you, Quinn? You've come back to take over your old man's place, I hear.'

Quinn wondered where Reg got his information from. He hadn't spoken to anyone before he talked to Braden only a few minutes ago. He avoided a direct answer. He didn't have one.

'I've been working up in the Territory on a big station out on the Barkley Tablelands, but the recent rains have put an end to that. Plus, I needed to come home and sort out Dad's stuff.'

'Will probably need a bit of sorting, hey?' Reg's eyes were shrewd.

'You sure keep a finger on the pulse, mate. And yeah, I've got a fair bit of sorting to do.'

Not that sorting was the right word, Quinn thought. As far as he could see there was no solution. What he needed was money and there was no possibility of that at the moment.

'I can imagine. Your old man spent a fair bit of time here in the pub before he went to the home and carked it. Sorry, I mean before he died.'

'That's okay, Reg. However you phrase it, Dad's gone. I'm back here now.'

'Here to stay?' The old bugger was persistent. Quinn shrugged. He knew whatever Reg was told, it would be around the town within minutes, probably before he even got back to the Landcruiser.

'Where else would I go? This is home,' he said, trying to give the impression that he would be staying. 'The Calthorpe family's been here for a hundred and fifty years.' He didn't want the word to get around that things were grim. That would happen soon enough.

'Staying, hey? Well, if you need to know anything you come and have a chat with me.'

'I will, Reg. Thanks, mate.'

Coming home to *Merry Downs* Station and seeing the empty paddocks, the broken fences, the pool full of green slimy water, and the biggest shock of all had almost broken Quinn.

Dad had been in hospital by then and he'd had one last visit with him a couple of days after he got home. He'd just made it; Dad passed away the same week.

He'd been pretty much incoherent when Quinn went to visit him, but he kept saying over and over, 'I'm sorry, son. I'm sorry, son. I couldn't do it after Vera died. I couldn't stay in the house. I'm sorry, but promise me, promise me you'll fix it up. It'll be fine, there's money there. Just use it.'

But the problem was there was no money there. There were no cattle, and the biggest shock of all— no house. He drove out to the back of the station and the old settler's cottage was still there; it looked like Dad had been living out there

All Quinn had was the money he'd managed to invest when he'd been in the Territory. Less the fifty grand he'd sent down when Dad had asked for a loan to buy some new steers. The problem was it was in a fixed-term investment, and he'd have to go back to Darwin to get his hands on some cash.

Life in the north had been good. The work was satisfying; he'd had a great boss working for a big pastoral company, and he'd managed to save. The group he worked with would head to Darwin on fishing weekends and they'd had one memorable trip up to Lorella Springs.

Coming back to the mess at Augathella, even though it was home, and it was where his heart was, had been a shock.

'Gone off with the pixies, boy?' Reg interrupted.

Quinn forced a laugh. 'Reg, I was just thinking about which way I was going to take a walk. I've had a couple of beers so I'm gonna go for a stroll before I drive home. I might go for a wander around town. See what's changed.'

'Not a lot to look at, but there's been a few changes. A new doctor and a new nurse at the hospital and a new accountant in town if you're looking for one. Damn good bloke he is too; he's the one who saved Peter Cartwright's life. He's moved in with that nice nurse. And he's setting up a little accountancy business from her spare room. You should give *him* a try.'

Quinn's eyes narrowed. Why was Reg harping about an accountant all of a sudden? What did he know?

'Dad's accountant is in Brisbane, mate.'

'Pfft,' came from Reg's lips. 'What would a city slicker in an office in Brisbane know about what you need to know out here?'

'That's true.' There was no point going into battle with Reg because he could be here for the afternoon.

'You need to get yourself a local fella.' Reg's expression was intent.

'I might go and see that bloke.' Quinn had some concerns about his father changing accountants just before he moved into the aged care facility. He'd asked Rob, his own accountant in Darwin, to check him out. He'd been trying to get onto the bloke in Brisbane for a couple of weeks.

'Good to welcome young ones to our town. He's a top young fella. Did a bit of everything before the truth came out.'

'The truth?' Quinn's curiosity won out over the inclination not to gossip.

'He was a drifter and a singer, and now he's the town hero. From what Braden Cartwright was saying, it looks like he's gonna get a few clients from here to Charleville because the old bloke down in Charleville who did their books has pulled the pin. He was your dad's accountant. Don't know how you ended up with a bloke in Brisbane.'

Neither did Quinn, but he wasn't going to tell Reg that.

'Rightio, mate. Time I was going. Thanks for bringing me up to speed with what's been going on.' Quinn picked up his hat from the table next to Reg where he'd left it on the way in, and headed off down Annie Street. He'd do the loop and then he'd pick up some groceries and head home.

As much as you could call the old settler's cottage home.

Chapter 4

Kimberley

The afternoon passed quickly. Kimberley glanced at her watch. It was heading for four o'clock by the time everyone had lunch, drinks were finished, and conversations were done. Time for her to get to school and prepare for Monday.

Petie Cartwright had curled up on Callie's lap and drifted off to sleep. Rory and Nigel were looking bored, sitting at the table and playing on an iPad. Braden stood up and tapped a fork on his glass.

'Thanks for coming in, everyone. I know it was short notice and we only decided when we came into town to have lunch here. It was great to see you all, and if I haven't thanked you personally, I just want to give another big thanks to everyone who looked out for us while we've been away. Thanks for the prayers. Thanks for the help, thanks for the food.' He glanced at Callie.

Tears filled her eyes as she lifted her head and spoke. 'Fallon just told me that I've got a freezer full of casseroles and cakes. You're a lovely bunch of friends. Thanks so much. We won't need to do a big shop much at IGA now, Bray.'

Kimberley turned as Jon Ingram's booming

laugh filled the room.

'Wait until you see your kitchen, Callie. When everyone heard you were coming home today, IGA was cleaned out. Everybody shopped and headed out to your place. You won't need to buy a carrot or a loaf of bread. In fact, you won't have room to even get into your kitchen.'

Callie's eyes welled again. Braden put his hand on her shoulder, and she reached up and took it. 'Thank you, everyone.' She looked up at Braden and Kimberley overheard her soft words. 'See I told you this is home, and this is where we're staying.'

Kim was surprised to hear that. She never thought that they might have considered moving away, but she guessed with a sick child you never knew what the outcome was going to be.

Braden and Callie gathered up the boys, and gradually everybody began to head home. Kim leaned over and said to Jacinta, 'I'm going to head back to school now. There are a couple of things I want to do. Make sure you see me before you leave, won't you?'

'I've got another two days at school. Bob begged me to stay for some of this week,' Jacinta said. 'Claudia wasn't available until Wednesday. She's working down at Morven. Anyway, what are you going to school for on a Sunday afternoon? Don't you have a home to go to?'

Kimberly laughed. 'I do, but I want to finish working on the staffing for next year.'

'Isn't that Bob's job?'

'It is, but between you and me, Bob's checked out a bit, so I thought it would do me good to get some experience.'

'You'll make a good principal there.'

'I have to get it first,' Kimberley said.

'You will. Everyone knows how good you are.'

Kimberly shook her head. 'The word is there's a transfer in the system. Looking to come out this way. It might not even go to ad.'

'Oh, surely not. People that want to transfer to those sorts of positions are usually second rate.' Jacinta frowned.

'Come on, be fair. You can't generalise.'

'Oh yes, I can. I've seen it, Kim. You deserve that job. You've been running the school all year.'

'Time will tell. I'll let you know what happens.'

##

Kimberly walked out to the car and as she unlocked the door, she noticed Quinn walking down the street towards the park.

Maybe to save a drive out she should catch him up and chat with him there. She stood, biting her lip for a moment, and then she thought that it would seem a bit too much. If she chased after him and tried to make conversation it would look strange.

Maybe.

It would be better if she dropped out to the station to welcome him home.

She frowned.

Wouldn't it?

Maybe it *would* be better to go and meet him down the street. Being Monday tomorrow, she was full up with a busy school week. Parent and Friends meeting, a couple of staff meetings, and then she was going to Charleville on Thursday for a professional development day. Or should she drive out this afternoon; there'd be time to get out there and back before dark.

Frustration filled Kimberley at her indecisiveness. It was not a trait that she usually encountered. The problem was she was so damned nervous about talking to Quinn. Not only because of the delicate nature of what she was worried about, but she was just nervous about talking to him after the way they had parted the night before he left town.

Maybe he wasn't going out to *Merry Downs* this afternoon? Now that he was hanging around town, she wondered if he was even out at the station. Maybe he was just visiting town and going away again. She should learn not to make assumptions.

Maybe *checking out* had an innocent meaning?

She frowned again, unsure of what to do, and then decided to speak to him now. As she hurried down the street to where Quinn had been walking, a white Landcruiser pulled out and drove away. Quinn was driving.

Right! She'd follow him and go and talk to him now. She would never forgive herself if she didn't and something happened. Opening the car door, she quickly slid in, started the engine and drove down the street, but by the time she got to the intersection, there was no sign of Quinn.

Maybe she should just not worry. He was a grown man. Maybe she hadn't heard what she thought she had. Taking a right at Bendee Street, she went around the block and headed down towards the school. She parked on the school grounds, put the key code in to let herself into the main office block and booted up her computer. But once she was settled at her desk, she couldn't focus on what she was doing. Her hands were shaking, and her stomach was churning.

Damn you, Quinn Calthorpe. All she could think about was him saying, 'I'm going to check out.' He hadn't looked like the Quinn she'd been such good friends with. A thought struck her. Maybe he wasn't well. Maybe that's what the problem was.

Kimberley turned her computer off, folded away the papers that she'd been trying to work on for the last half hour and headed back out to her car. She knew what he drove, and she'd keep an eye out as she went through town. If she didn't go and talk to him, she'd never forgive herself if the unthinkable happened. She couldn't even bring herself to think of it.

She turned down Nelson Street and back past the pub, but there was no sign of Quinn or his vehicle. There was nothing else open in town this afternoon. She even did a second circuit around the pub to make sure he wasn't there, and Reg gave her a wave and a curious look. As far as Kimberley knew, Quinn had no family in town, so she headed out along Roselyn Road. Hopefully, he'd gone back out to the station.

She'd drive out to *Merry Downs.*

If he wasn't there, at least she'd tried. It was a pleasant afternoon for a drive through the bush. She hadn't been out this way for years.

Her thoughts were jumbled as she drove. Old memories of pleasant afternoons with Quinn, picnics in the bush, Saturday mornings at the coffee shops and the occasional swim in the *Merry Downs* pool. She hadn't ever felt comfortable being out there. Kim knew, back in those days she didn't make it socially. His mother, Vera, had been the mistress of disapproving looks, and icy cold politeness. It was sad but there was only Quinn left; his parents had both passed.

Now her only problem was to think of a reason for driving out there.

Half an hour later Kimberley shook her head as she turned onto the road that took her past Craig Wilson's place. It seemed like ages since Sophie stayed with her and they'd caught the bus to the Easter concert at the Wilson property. Now Sophie and Kent were married and finally away on their honeymoon.

What to say to Quinn if he was there.

And if he wasn't, she'd worry about what to do then.

I don't need a reason to visit. Simply an old friend coming to say hello. Or how about even being honest? She was a friend, and she was concerned about him, and if he didn't like that, well, he could lump it.

I couldn't help but overhear your phone conversation at the bar, Quinn, and it worried me. Is there anything I can do to help?

Yes, that would do. Short, succinct, and caring.

I can do it.

If she could stand up at a regional staff development meeting and talk to two hundred teachers, she could take on one man who used to be

40

her friend.

Her mouth dried as she passed the Wilson place, and she knew it wasn't too much further to *Merry Downs*.

At one stage nerves took hold and she felt sick in the stomach; she gripped the wheel with sweaty hands and talked herself out of turning around.

All the way out, she thought about her relationship with Quinn and how they had become such close friends. But they'd blown it, and she wished she could go back to that last night and make a different decision.

When Jacinta had asked hadn't they been an item once, she'd brushed it off. Up until a couple of years ago Kimberley knew she still had feelings for him, but Quinn had moved away to the ,Northern Territory. It hadn't broken her heart, but she'd gotten over it. Time was a great healer, and not having any contact with him let her forget him.

Mind you, she had been excited when she heard he'd come back to town, even though they had parted under such awkward circumstances. Seeing him in the pub today had been a shock; he looked so different. She hadn't felt comfortable going up and speaking to him when everyone else was there and happy, and it was a very social occasion.

Finally, the *Merry Downs* sign appeared in the distance. Kimberly slowed as she approached the main gates. The entrance looked strangely dilapidated—almost abandoned. Mr Calthorpe had always taken great pride in his station being a showpiece from the front gate to the back paddocks; it was sad to see it looking neglected. The sign that had once hung over the ornate front gates was hanging drunkenly to one side, and the chain on the east side swayed in the afternoon wind. The gates were rusted, and one hung crookedly off the hinges.

It was hard to believe this was the station she had visited in her teens, but when she thought about it, that was almost twelve years ago, and a lot could happen in that time.

She was pleased to see the dust hanging above the driveway as she drove through the gates. That meant Quinn had only been a little way ahead of her, and it had been his dust she'd followed.

He was home.

Her hands shook as she changed back a gear and she turned into the property and slowed as she negotiated the rutted driveway. From memory, it was about a kilometre down to the house. As a teenager in the excitement of coming to the property, she hadn't taken that much notice. Kimberley looked around as she drove. There was no sign of any cattle, even though the pasture was long and green. She was surprised Quinn didn't have a mob on there at the moment.

When Kimberly steered her little hatchback around the last curve before Calthorpe Homestead her foot slammed on the brake as she stared ahead. Her mouth dropped open, and she blinked in disbelief.

There was no homestead.

The beautiful building was gone; where it had once been was new growth of low, mulga scrub with a brick chimney rearing up to the sky on the righthand side.

Why would the house be gone? She hadn't heard anything about that. What on earth could have happened?

She stared ahead; the dust trail from Quinn's car was further down the road.

Shaking her head in shock, Kimberley put the car back into drive and as she drove slowly past the side of the once-beautiful homestead, she looked to the left and stopped where the back gate had once been. All that was left was the pool fence and the high rock wall that the boys had once dived off. From what she could see from the car, the pool was still there, but it didn't appear to have any water in it.

The house that had been known as one of the best in the district had been a double-storey construction of six bedrooms, even though Quinn was an only child. The other rooms had always been

43

full of guests on the occasions that Kimberley had visited, but she or Beth had never been invited to stay.

How could something once so beautiful have been let go like this? The outdoor area with rolling green lawns and the massive pool lay derelict. The shed covering the pump from the bore that had watered the lawn and filled the pool was half gone and the exposed pipes were twisted and rusted.

A wave of sadness engulfed her. If she felt like this, how must Quinn feel?

The only thing left on the whole site was the pool and it still had the safety fence around it. She wondered how long the house had been gone and what had happened, but by the state of the site, it looked like it had been like that for a while. Maybe that was why Quinn looked so miserable, but surely it wasn't enough motivation to say what he had.

Accelerating a little, she followed the dirt road in the direction Quinn had gone.

If it hadn't been for the slight puff of dust a long distance ahead, she wouldn't have known what to do, but she soldiered on stoically and followed the road, wondering where he was going and what she would find out there.

After another ten kilometres, Kimberly slowed her car as she crested a slight rise. The white Landcruiser was parked next to an old house at the bottom of the hill.

Not just an old house, but what appeared to be an original settler's cottage. The rusted roof glowed in dirty blood-red shadow. On this side of the building, the sagging roof overhanging the narrow verandah was propped up by a timber post sitting at an awkward angle.

Kimberly's throat tightened as she drove slowly through the open gate and looked around as she approached Quinn's car. There was no sign of him, but a red kelpie barked and came running from the back of the house as she pulled in behind the Landcruiser.

The sun was low in the sky, and even though the house was a ramshackle dump, the afternoon sun was kind, giving a beautiful pink glow to the faded brown weatherboards.

She climbed out of the car and the kelpie nipped at her ankles, but she was used to being on farms and she gave it a quick command to sit, and it did. She'd had the air conditioning on all the way from town, and when she stepped out, the heat of the afternoon sun hit her like a brick.

The grass around the house was long and lush especially around a small lean-to shed coming off the back. A couple of rusted fridges and freezers, obviously years past their use-by date, filled the small space. Long grass grew around them and a pile of old timber ran along the side wall of the shed.

She shivered. A snake haven. If there was one thing that scared her it was snakes.

The front door was open, or rather she should say the front doorway, as there appeared to be no door hanging on the hinges at the side of the open space. As Kimberley approached the house, she hesitated, unsure whether to go towards the house or look around in the sheds that were scattered around the fenced block. Maybe Quinn had just come out here to the station to get something? Or to feed the dog? No one could possibly live here.

Or did Quinn? The thought that he was indeed living here crossed her mind. She shook her head again and walked slowly towards the front veranda supported by another two posts at a drunken lean; the roof was almost touching the ground at one corner. A curtain of cobwebs filled the space, and she came to a sudden stop. The guttering hung off the roof and the downpipe was lying on the ground next to the space that had once held the front door.

The kelpie trotted along beside her, letting out the occasional sharp bark as if to ask her what she wanted, and as she approached the doorway, Quinn appeared.

'What are you barking—?' He broke off and his body tensed when he saw Kimberly and looked over towards her car. His expression held not a glimmer of a smile to welcome her.

'Wow. it's hot out here,' she said as he stood there glaring at her.

'What do you want, Kimmy?'

'It's Kimberley these days, Quinn.' Her tone was placatory. 'I thought that I'd come and visit you. I wanted to talk to you.'

'Visit me? Why? What do you want? Why did you follow me out here? If you wanted to say hello you could've come and said gidday at the pub.'

'Yes, I could have I know, but it was pretty busy with Petie, and Jacinta and I were talking to everyone and catching up. As I left I saw you go for a walk and I was going to catch you up, but by the time I drove down there was no sign of you.'

His lips were set in a straight line, and he folded his arms. 'Why did you want to catch me? What did you want to talk to me about?'

'What happened to the old house? What happened to your home?' She couldn't help her eyes filling with moisture and she swallowed. This was not the place she remembered, and this was not the man she had once known very well. As much as a woman could ever know a man. She pushed that memory away; they had been coming back too much today.

'I said, what do you want?'

'I was—' Kimberley hesitated, unsure of what to say. His attitude was certainly not conducive to a heart-to-heart talk.

'You were what?'

'Okay.' She drew herself to her full height, which at five foot three was not very high, and put her hands on her hips. 'I came out here because when I saw you in the pub this afternoon, I was concerned about you.'

'What the hell gave you a reason to be concerned? And what gives you the right to follow me out here?'

She removed her hands from her hips and gestured to him. 'Look at you. You look like you haven't eaten for a month, and you look absolutely miserable. We were friends once, Quinn, and I thought I could express my concern to you, but I'm obviously not welcome. It's hot out here. Perhaps can we go inside out of the sun?'

'I'd rather not,' Quinn said. 'I've got things to do.'

Her eyes widened at the anger and tension in his tone.

'Well, perhaps we could sit on the veranda?' she asked.

Quinn must have seen the colour of her face, and he shrugged and walked slowly up the two front steps. He gestured to a chair that had seen better days. Foam rubber was poking through the cracked vinyl. 'Just move your hand over it. It'll get rid of the loose stuff and it won't stick to your legs.'

This time she raised her eyebrows as she ran a hand over the chair and gingerly sat down.

'Thank you. It's much cooler here in the shade.' Her tone was formal.

His manners obviously got the better of him. 'Would you like a drink of water? You are flushed.' A shade of the old Quinn surfaced briefly.

'That would be most welcome, Quinn. Thank you.'

Kimberly looked around at the green paddocks surrounding the old house. The afternoon sun bathed the trees in a warm glow. The yard in front of the house was bare; the grass here had obviously died in the recent drought.

Quinn's mum had always taken great pride in her garden at the homestead and a landscaper from Charleville had looked after it.

Kimberley was beginning to understand what was wrong with Quinn. She looked up as he came out and handed her a large glass of iced water, and then sat on the chair across from hers.

He didn't worry about brushing it first. 'I'm quite busy this afternoon, Kimberley, so I can't be very social and entertain you. Perhaps you could finish your drink and tell me why you've come out here.'

'I just wanted to see how you're going; it's been such a long time. Welcome you back to town and all that.'

'And all that?' Quinn raised his eyebrows and looked at her. 'What's all that?'

'For goodness' sake, Quinn. We were good mates once. Can't I just come out for a Sunday afternoon drive to say gidday and welcome home?' Her hand was shaking and she put the glass on the floor beside the chair

'Home?' His voice was flat.

'Yes. Home.'

'Like I said before, you could've said gidday at the pub. There's nothing out here anymore. No social events, no *friends*.'

'Is that what's bothering you?'

He seemed to recede into himself for a moment before he answered. 'What do you mean? What's bothering me?'

Kimberley swallowed and wondered whether to be honest. 'I couldn't help overhearing you on the phone when I was waiting at the bar with Jacinta.'

'Eavesdropping these days, are we? That's not a very good way to teach your students at school.'

'Oh, so you know I'm a teacher, do you?'

'Just because I live out here and just because I've been away doesn't mean I don't know what's happening in town.'

***

Quinn knew he was being a right proper bastard, but he didn't know what Kimmy Riordan was doing out here. It was too close for comfort. He looked around. She glared at him when he'd said his piece and he stared back.

Kimberley had grown into a very attractive woman. Her brunette hair touched her shoulders with a slight curl, and her brown eyes were clear and wide. Her cheeks still held a flush, and her pretty lips were touched with soft pink lipstick. Her figure was as slim as it had always been; it was hard to believe she was heading for thirty. She still looked the same as she had at eighteen when he'd last seen her. He glanced down at her hands; she wore no rings, but that didn't mean anything these days.

Quinn jerked his thoughts into gear. There was no point going back to those memories, friendships or more.

She ignored his last words. 'So, I came out here because I was concerned about you. Why did you say what you did? Why do you look so bad? Are you ill?' She hesitated and he guessed she'd heard him talk about checking out.

He chuckled. 'You overheard words and you put

your own meaning on them. Must come from teaching grammar and vocabulary.' He deliberately kept his voice hard and his expression bland. He wouldn't get back into any sort of relationship with Kimberley, no matter how tempting it was. 'Checking out? That's what you heard me say.'

'Yes.' Her voice was soft and again he looked at her, thinking how beautiful she was.

'There's no need to worry about me, Kimberley. I'm a big boy now, and yes, I've got my problems, but you don't need to bother about them. It was good to see you, but I've got a lot of stuff to do this evening.' He stood and took the glass of water that she hadn't touched.

The flush on her cheeks deepened and he felt mean.

'I'm sorry. You haven't touched the water.' He went to hand it back.

'No, don't bother. You probably don't want to associate with an interfering eavesdropper. I wasn't doing it deliberately. I'm sorry I've wasted your time. I hope you have a good life. Goodbye, Quinn.'

She jumped up and hurried down the front steps while he stood there holding the full glass. The car door slammed and the wheels spun in the red dust as she roared up the road. He stood there for a long time, watching the dust settle after she disappeared over the hill.

Bluey came over and rubbed his head against Quinn's thigh.

'Well, that went well, didn't it, Blue?'

Chapter 5

Quinn

On Wednesday, Quinn called into the hospital to meet with Dr Higgins to see if he could shed any light on what his father had done.

'Hello, Quinn. Good to meet you.' Dr Higgins held out his hand.

'Dr Higgins.' Quinn shook the proffered hand.

'Harry, please. I'm sorry I didn't see you before your father passed, but I was away at a conference the week you were here.'

'All good.'

'Have a seat.' Harry led him over to two armchairs at the side of the office. Once they were seated, he asked, 'Now how can I help you?'

Quinn shook his head. 'Where to start?'

'The beginning.' Harry smiled encouragingly.

'I'm in a mess. Or rather the station is in a mess. There's no records, no money and worst of all, no house.'

'No house?'

'I think it was burned down. I went into town and saw the fire blokes and they had no idea. I went next door and saw Craig Wilson, and he didn't know either, so it's a bit of a mystery. I asked them not to say anything because I don't want it getting around. Did my father talk to you at all about the property?'

Harry frowned. 'No, never. Your father was totally focused on the loss of your mother. We never spoke of a station. In fact, I wasn't even aware he was on the land. He told me he was a bricklayer.'

Quinn's eyes widened. 'Really? Dad wouldn't know the first thing about that. He was an excellent cattleman; he was born on the land, and lived all his life on it.'

'Dementia is a cruel thing, Quinn. You're aware that your father had a stroke and that's why he was in the hospital when you came down?'

'Yes, I was.'

'He was fortunate that he didn't have physical issues from the stroke. It was a frontal lobe stroke, and that's what caused his dementia. We call that form vascular dementia. There are various stages of cognitive decline, but unfortunately, his onset was sudden and severe. All we talked about was Vera and how he didn't want to live without her. Sounds like he was making good decisions before the stroke. I believe his wife, your mum, passed away twelve months ago.'

'That's right. I came back from Darwin the last week or two before Mum died. Dad was fine then; of course, he was grief-stricken about Mum, knowing that she didn't have long, but the property was in a great state. He had a couple of blokes working for him. He'd come out of the drought and the place looked really good. The house was still there. After I went back, I'd call him every couple of weeks, and we'd have a yarn.'

'And no one can shed any light on what happened. The neighbours? His mates?'

Quinn hesitated. 'You'd have to understand my parents. Mum was from Sydney and even though she lived out here for a long time, she didn't have much to do with the local community. I believe she also isolated Dad over the years, so no local mates, and the neighbours had nothing to do with them. It was one of the reasons I moved away. I was a great disappointment to my mother. I refused to go to boarding school in Sydney, and I passed on going to university. I guess my genes came from my father's side. I just wanted to be on the land. I came home to take over the property, but I'm not going to be able to.'

'Why is that?'

Quinn shrugged. 'A few months ago. I might have said yes. When his solicitor in Sydney rang me to let me know that Dad had left me all the property, I wasn't surprised. I was an only child. Dad's brother is still alive and I half-expected that he might have given him a share, but I was the sole recipient.'

'Sounds like your father wanted you home. The solicitor couldn't enlighten you on anything?'

'No. All he had was the will. No other documents.'

'So you don't want to stay and make a go of it?'

He looked up and met the doctor's kind eyes. 'I honestly don't know if I've got the energy to start. I certainly don't have the finances. So I have to decide what to do about the station itself and what to do about cattle and paddocks or crops?'

'What sort of station was it?'

'Sheep and cattle, but there's no livestock at all. No house, no stock, no fences.' Quinn leaned forward, dangling his hands between his knees. 'And worst of all, as far as I can see, there's no money to start afresh. I always looked forward to coming home and running the place myself. That's the main reason I went to the Northern Territory; to get some experience, try some new ideas and get my helicopter pilot's licence. I was going to do my own mustering. Bit hard to do that when there's no stock.'

'I'm sorry I couldn't shed any light on the mystery for you. I'll go back through my predecessor's notes and see if I can see anything there. I guess you've got some big decisions to make.'

'I sure do.' Quinn's throat closed as he thought

of the issues he had to deal with.

'One thing I will say to you, Quinn. It's very clear to me from the way you've spoken that this is where you want to be and that you're struggling a fair bit. Don't rush into any decision, and if you'd like someone to talk to, don't hesitate to make an appointment and talk with me again.'

Quinn stood. 'Thanks, doc. I'll take that advice on board.'

Chapter 6

Kim was still out of sorts on Thursday morning when she pulled up at the state school just after seven. It had taken the whole trip back to town on Sunday to calm down. She felt like a fool.

An interfering, eavesdropping fool.

She was always the first to arrive at school these days. Bob Hamblin had been a dedicated principal, but over the course of this school year, he seemed to have lost interest in the school and turned up just before bell time every morning. Kim was usually there by herself for a good half hour each day, with only the cleaners to keep her company before the first teachers arrived.

This morning she checked for phone messages, and unsuccessfully tried to source a casual teacher to replace a sick Year Six teacher. Being back in routine soothed her frazzled nerves. She'd been fine when she went home from school and meetings each day this week, but when she'd had time to herself to sit and think at home each night, she still couldn't get Quinn out of her thoughts.

She had to.

After checking her email, Kim went to the hall to say hello to Helen and Louise, the two cleaners, before going to the staffroom kitchen to make her second coffee of the morning. Then she was heading down to Charleville for a professional development course on student well-being. Maybe she'd learn something about *adult* well-being and when to pull her head in.

The door opened and Kim turned around, surprised that someone else was in so early. Callie Cartwright walked in.

'Morning, Kim.'

'Hi, Callie. Is everything okay? You're early today.'

'I'm fine, thanks. I've just got a heap of preparation to do after being away for so long. Braden's bringing the boys into town this morning. He's got a meeting in Charleville this afternoon, and he won't be home tonight, so he thought he'd have some extra time with them this morning.'

'He's a good dad.'

'He is.'

'Is Petie coming back to kindy today seeing Braden's away?'

'No, we're not sending him back for a couple of weeks yet. We still need to keep an eye on him and keep his head protected. Mind you, it's hard to keep him quiet with two brothers and three dogs in the house. But to their credit, Rory and Nigel have been really good with him. I think witnessing the accident has traumatised both of them to some extent. Petie's going to Ruth today.'

'I thought she was out at Fallon and Jon's house at the back of your station.'

'No, Ruth and Jeff have bought a small house in Annie Street. They're getting ready for when little Ryan comes to school.'

'Wow, that's forward planning. I didn't know that.'

'They moved in a couple of weeks ago. I don't think they'll go back to the coast. Fallon's going to start flying again soon, and Ruth will be here to babysit when she does. Did you know Fallon and Jon bought a place out near Craig Wilson's? They'll be moving from our old house soon.'

Kim's head flew up and she dropped the teaspoon she'd been stirring her coffee with.

'Near the Wilsons? Not *Merry Downs*?'

'I don't know the station name. I just know it borders Craig's property.'

'Okay.' Kim didn't want to say any more. It was none of her business if Quinn sold up. 'It's so good to have you back at school.'

'Do you always get here this early?' Callie looked at her quizzically.

'I do, but you just remember I haven't got three little boys, a house and assorted pets to look after, plus I only live a couple of streets away. I walk to and from school most days; it clears my head on the

61

way home.'

'You still live around the corner?'

'I do, but I didn't walk today because I've got an in-service in Charleville.' She pulled a face and lifted one foot. 'Thus, the heels.'

'You look very professional in your suit,' Callie said with a smile.

'Have to create the image.'

Kim and Callie had struck up a friendship before Callie started work at the school. Sophie had introduced them, and they had a lot in common. Callie was a good teacher and had not only settled into the school well but had quickly become a part of the local community. Everyone had been really happy when she and Braden had fallen for each other and eloped.

It was also good to see how happy Braden was these days, and now that Petie was recovering from the accident at Sophie and Kent's wedding, life was back on an even keel for the Cartwrights.

'I wouldn't leave *Kilcoy Station*, but sometimes it would be nice not to have that drive into town. I really need to catch up on what I've missed with the kids here while we've been away.'

'Grab your cuppa and we'll have a quick chat.' Kim glanced at her watch. 'I've got half an hour before I have to leave.' She took her cuppa to the table in the centre of the room and waited for Callie to join her.

'So let's start with my class. Although I do like to know about any other kids who need some extra care so I can keep an eye on any problems when I'm on playground duty and sport.'

'Okay, let's start with your class. We've had a few problems with Jarod Evans. His parents have split and he's not coping really well. Mum's ex has moved to Charleville for work and his uncle has come back to town for a while. He seems to be a bit of a bad influence. Jared's been swearing in class and is being rough with the smaller kids. Keep an eye on him when you're on duty too.'

Callie frowned. 'I don't know his family, but is his mother Ros Evans?'

Kim nodded. 'Do you know her?'

'I know of her. It was her brother Sophie lived with for a while before she got back with Kent.'

'Ah. I wasn't aware of that connection. He must be the uncle who's come back to town.'

Callie frowned. 'I hope it doesn't cause any problems for Sophie and Kent when they get home from their honeymoon.'

'I'm sure it won't. Anyway, keep an eye on Jared and if he gets into any rough stuff, send him to me. Or to Bob, if I'm away.'

Kim mentioned a few other students who needed a bit of extra attention. 'If you have any problems today, ask Jacinta. She's here for another couple of days.'

'I will. How's the Christmas concert planning going?' Callie asked.

'We're about to start that, so it's really good to have you back this week. Claudia's volunteered but she'd been really enthusiastic.' Callie raised her eyebrows and Kim chuckled. 'I know. She can be overly enthusiastic about everything, but her heart is in the right place.'

'She'll be fine. We can all pitch in. The boys are really excited about it. Since they entered the Easter Eisteddfod there's been no stopping them. They even have impromptu concerts at home now.' Callie wrapped her hands around her coffee mug and smiled. 'It's *so* good to be home and back to normal.'

'It's wonderful to have you back, Callie. We were all so worried about Petie.'

'This is the most incredible community, you know,' Callie said. 'We had so much support when we were in Brisbane and the number of friends who turned up at the pub on Sunday afternoon blew me away.'

'The Cartwright family are an institution in this town,' Kim said. 'We supported Braden when Julia was killed, we helped Sophie out when she was looking after the boys, and now it's just so good to see you guys back to normal.' Kim smiled. 'A little bird told me there's another Cartwright on the way.'

'Yes, the news is getting out around town. We're all really excited.'

'When do Sophie and Kent get back?'

'They've decided since they were delayed by Petie's accident, they're going to have a little bit longer away. Sophie emailed us last night. They're coming home via Cairns, and hiring a car and they're going to drive down the coast for a couple of weeks. Jon's keeping an eye on *Lara Waters.*'

'They deserve it,' Kim said. 'I'm so pleased to see Sophie happily married.'

'What about you? Are you still focusing all your attention on school? You know you need to have balance.' Callie put her coffee mug down.

'I'm okay. This is my life here at school. It's where I spend most of my time.'

Callie shook her head. 'You need to be careful, love. Don't get too immersed in your work. You need another interest in your life.'

Quinn Calthorpe popped straight into Kim's thoughts as he had done all week. She'd lost sleep over the past few nights, worrying about him, and worrying about how she'd left in a temper.

'Another interest?' she said slowly. 'I do have something on my mind. I've been a bit preoccupied this week, and I could do with some female advice,

Callie.'

'Fire away.'

'I have a friend who I think is struggling. I went out to see him after lunch last Sunday because I was worried about something I overheard him say, even though I had no right to be listening. He was really rude to me, and I lost my temper and left, but the more I think about it, the more I'm starting to think he was deliberately rude so I would go away. That worries me. I don't think he's in a very good headspace at the moment. I've been worried about him all week. I don't know his number and I don't think there's phone service out there anyway.'

'So what advice do you need?'

'Should I persevere, or should I leave him in peace? Is it any of my business? I don't know if you know Quinn. Quinn Calthorpe?'

'I haven't met him, but I know Braden's giving him a lift to that meeting tonight.'

'That's good to hear. Maybe he'll talk to Braden.'

Callie raised her eyebrows. 'You think so? Men are different to us, Kim. They keep stuff to themselves.'

'I know. I think he might be suffering from depression. He looks dreadful, and I heard him say something that really worried me. Have you ever heard the phrase "checking out"?'

'Yes, I know what it can mean. Do you really think he's that depressed, Kim?'

'I don't know. I don't know if I'm interfering in my usual student well-being mindset, or whether I should be worried.'

'It sounds like you were a good friend, and you went to check on somebody you were worried about. I think you did the right thing, even though his reaction wasn't what you hoped for. If you're really worried about him, is there someone else you can talk to? Someone else who knows him. I'm sort of in the dark as to what to tell you, because I don't know him.'

Kim nodded slowly. 'I could call my sister, Beth. They were in the same year and good mates.'

'Maybe you can talk to her and see what she reckons if she knows him that well.'

'Thank you, Callie. Talking it out helps me see the problem from a different perspective.'

'Any time. Anyway, it's about time I headed to the classroom. I need to get myself sorted before the kids arrive.'

'And I'm off to a meeting in Charleville. You have a good day.' Kim rinsed her cup and went back to her office to check her email before she left.

She'd text Beth and see if she was free. They could chat on speakerphone while she was on the way to Charleville.

Chapter 7

Callie yawned as she reached for the paints on the top shelf in her classroom.

She'd shoved them up there earlier in the day, when the kids had finished their wet painting, and she knew she had to clean them up before they dried. Feeling slightly uncomfortable, she took a deep breath and stretched. A sharp cramp grabbed near her left hip, and she bent double.

Holding her side with one hand and breathing evenly, she closed her eyes until the cramp went away; it had felt like a piece of elastic stretching until it had no more give, and she was worried that something was going to break.

'Oh, no, don't let it be the baby. Please God, don't let it be the baby.'

The kids from her class had all gone out to the bus and she had only thought to fill the time before she went to get the boys from tennis coaching and collected Petie from Ruth's place.

Once the pain has eased, she sat down and waited; it had stopped and hadn't come back. Maybe she'd just pulled a muscle from stretching. She swallowed and realised she was worrying too much.

She'd leave the paint out until tomorrow; it

would last a day or so, and she would make herself a cup of coffee and have a sit-down and stop worrying about every little twinge and cramp.

On her way to the kitchen, Callie detoured via the bathroom because something just didn't feel right.

It's only my overactive imagination, she told herself, but her throat closed when she noticed the bright stain on her undies. Her eyes filled with tears as her heart began to pound.

Grabbing a wad of toilet paper, she tidied herself and made her way to the kitchen and sat down just as Claudia came into the room.

'You okay, Mrs Cartwright? You're a bit pale.'

Callie shook her head, and her voice shook when she spoke. 'Claudia, can you drop me down to the hospital? I've got a bit of a problem. I think I might be having a miscarriage. I need to see Dr Higgins or Laura.'

Claudia's eyes widened and she came over and put her arm around Callie. 'Do you want me to call an ambulance instead?'

'No, just put me in your car and take me down to the hospital.'

Claudia supported her as they walked to the door.

Chapter 8

Quinn

Quinn forced a smile to his face as he took his hat off and climbed into the back of Braden's Landcruiser.

Craig Wilson turned around from the front passenger seat. 'G'day, mate, haven't seen you since your dad's funeral. How's it going?'

'Can't complain,' Quinn said with a forced grin. There was no point whingeing. He'd been reluctant to travel in the car down to Charleville with them, but he couldn't think of a good excuse to say no when Braden called.

'Crazy to take three vehicles when we're all going to the same place,' Braden said. 'And at the town hall, parking is always scarce when everyone turns up at the meetings.'

'Fair enough,' Quinn agreed reluctantly. There was really no point going to the meeting, but who knew what might come out of it? He'd keep an ear to the ground and see if anyone was looking for property. Word of mouth was still the main way properties sold.

They'd organised to meet at the pub at Augathella, and Braden had pulled up as Quinn got out of his vehicle.

Because he was in the back with the road noise,

and the radio on in the front, it was hard for Quinn to hear what Braden and Craig were chatting about in the front as they sped down the highway towards Charleville, so he leaned back and looked out the window at the passing landscape.

If only he had some cattle, he thought. He'd never seen the paddocks so green and lush out here. Grass was growing along the side of the hot bitumen, and even the trees looked healthy and moist.

So much for the brown and red outback during the drought; there wasn't a patch of red dirt to be seen.

'What do you reckon?' Craig asked, turning around to Quinn again.

'Sorry I can't hear very well back here.'

Braden leaned forward and turned the radio off. 'Craig and I were just talking about the new breed that Jon's been experimenting with, out at Kent Mason's place. Do you know much about them?'

Quinn nodded. 'Actually, I do. I was talking to Kent on the phone before I came down from the Territory. It's a breed that was introduced up there a few months back. I worked with them on one of the big stations near Victoria River.'

'And how do you reckon they'd go down here?'

'At the moment, good, but they'd also do well in the dry. They're certainly not going to suffer with the amount of water and grass that's around at the moment.'

Craig nodded. 'Yeah. What a season, hey? It's like Christmas every day.'

'As long as we don't get the floods they've had up around Barky and Longreach,' Braden said.

'True, we don't need any more rain,' Quinn agreed, even though none of that affected him at the moment. He sank back into his thoughts. He'd spent the week on the phone when he had service at the station and had driven into town a couple of times to get on the computer at the library and send some emails. The phone and internet service at *Merry Downs* was crap and he couldn't rely on emails coming through.

He'd made no progress, although he had established that dad *had* definitely been with the accountant at Charleville up until a few months before he died. He tried to call the accountant in Brisbane again to see what the gist of his changing over was, but the phone rang out and went to voicemail, which left him with a slightly uncomfortable feeling. He must give Mike a call and see if he'd been able to find anything out.

He'd also made no progress on establishing what had happened to the house. It was hard to see if it had burnt down, or if it had been demolished. He'd walked around the site of the homestead a few times. Surely there would have been rubbish from either a fire or a demolition? There was nothing but long lush grass and the single chimney standing. That pointed to a fire, but why didn't he know about it? The airstrip was overgrown and there was no sign of Dad's plane.

When he'd come out here after he'd seen Dad in hospital, it appeared he'd been living in the old settler's cottage.

When he'd asked him about the house and the Cessna, Dad had looked at him blankly. Quinn couldn't find the insurance papers or any paperwork. No cattle records. Nothing. But he guessed that all the paperwork had gone with the house. There was a lot to be said for technology; he stored all his personal documents in the cloud. Scanned and securely stored so he could access wherever he was. It just annoyed him that he had to go back to the bank in Darwin in person to access his investment.

Quinn leaned his head back as his thoughts churned. To top it all off, as well as making all the calls and worrying about what he was going to do, he couldn't forget Kim's visit on Sunday.

He had been rude to her, but he didn't want her hanging around, giving her his sympathy because that was his Achilles heel. He needed to focus, and he was determined to get out of this mess. He needed to find out what had happened and if there was actually any money left. Even though he had his investment, he didn't have enough to start again, and he didn't want to borrow against the unknown.

If he let Kim back into his heart—and that would be very easy to do since she'd never left it— he wouldn't be able to focus. They'd had such a solid friendship before he'd stuffed it up that last day they'd spent together at Paradise Springs before he'd headed off to the Northern Territory.

Seemed crazy that a woman he hadn't seen or spoken to in over eleven years had stayed in his head—and his heart. Sure, he'd had relationships over the past years. But always casual flings, nothing that ever tempted permanency.

As soon as she'd walked into the pub on Sunday, his internal radar had picked her up, and he hadn't been surprised when he'd seen her at the bar. He'd known she was back in town, and running into her would be inevitable.

His morose mood, exacerbated by a couple of beers and hearing that Mike couldn't get onto Dad's accountant had given him the strength to pretend he hadn't even seen her.

When she turned up at the station that evening, he'd been stunned, and he'd almost given in and told her what was going on.

But it was none of Kim's business. He knew

nothing about her now.

She'd grown up and her flash of temper as she'd left had surprised him. The Kim of old would have wheedled and spoken to him softly until he cracked and by God, he'd been close to cracking that day.

He'd dreamed about her for the past four nights and had woken up with a smile on his face until reality came flooding back with the morning sunlight streaming through the gaps of the old dwelling. Quinn knew he'd been out of line.

Next time he saw her, he'd apologise. He had been immature. He didn't have to spill his guts and tell her all his problems, but they had been good friends, and he needed to make amends for his rudeness.

He just wouldn't get too close; she was the one woman who could get into his heart, and he had nothing to offer her.

If he'd come home to a working station with cattle, and a decent house, he would have something to offer her. He had the work ethic and the knowledge to make a success of a station. He would've searched her out to catch up with her. He suspected she wasn't married, but he couldn't be sure; maybe he'd try and slip that into the conversation with Braden after the meeting.

His spirits had come up a little bit since he'd seen Kim and his world was looking a bit brighter;

there were good people around here. He would have a chat with Braden later and seek his advice.

Quinn had made some very low-key enquiries around town without saying anything about the house. After speaking to Craig Wilson, and the RFS, he'd mentioned his return to *Merry Downs* at the post office and at the bank, but it appeared that no one knew that the homestead had gone and that surprised him.

As they approached the outskirts of Charleville, Quinn pushed everything from his mind, he would try to get back to being reasonable and even-tempered, and maybe he'd learn something at this meeting today. Then this weekend, he'd go into town and seek Kim out. He was sure Braden would know where she lived.

Quinn's spirits plummeted again, listening to Craig and Braden discussing their herds and their plans for the winter as they walked towards the town hall.

Quinn was already regretting coming; it was probably going to be a waste of time, but then again, it was better than sitting in that building or wasting money at the pub.

'Looks like we're early enough,' Braden said. 'Let's sit up the front. I can never hear old Joe Miller when he gets up. He won't use the microphone because he doesn't like those new-fangled things!'

Craig chuckled. 'Tell us something Joe Miller does like.'

'A beer.' Braden grinned.

Quinn's feet dragged as they walked along the footpath to the town hall. Braden and Craig continue to chat beside him and he switched off.

He shook himself mentally. 'Stop worrying,' he told himself. 'It's not the end of the world. I've got 5000 acres of prime land and a lot of people would give their right arm for that.'

If only he could afford to get some stock and build the place up, he could put up with living in the old shack. It was no worse than camping out when he was mustering on the Barkly Tablelands. With some finance, he could start slow. Fixing the fences and getting a small herd would be a good start, but since he'd sent that money to Dad, the remainder of Quinn's investment wouldn't cover what was needed.

The only way to do it was to find out what had happened and find the plane, and the rest of the money. Plus, there was some money coming back from the aged care facility, he had discovered. Not a lot, but every cent would help.

When they were settled in the fourth row from

the front of the hall, Brayden leaned over and spoke to him.

'Might be something here of interest today, mate. Joe Miller was telling me about a couple of government-funded traineeships if you need any stockmen. Young help on your property that won't cost you anything.'

A spark of interest flared in Quinn.

Craig was talking to the Mitchell fellow from Tambo on the other side of him, and Quinn turned to Braden. 'Thanks for that info, but I need to be honest. I don't know why I came down here with you. Today was probably a waste of time. I'm going to be walking off *Merry Downs,* I think.'

Braden's eyes widened. 'Walking off? What do you mean?'

'Leaving. Checking out and heading back to the Territory. Working for wages.'

'But it's your family property, Quinn. I thought you loved it here. I thought you only went away to get some experience.'

'That was the plan. But it looks like things aren't going to work out that way.'

'Let's chat over a beer later,' Braden said. 'Here come those government blokes. Better pay attention.'

Chapter 9

Kim

Kim sat in the back row of the auditorium at the racecourse and listened to the speaker drone on. Some of these days were really worthwhile, and she would come away with new knowledge and motivation, but occasionally, a dud speaker would be invited. She could tell at this session that most of the teachers and executive members had switched off. What the department head from Brisbane was talking about was completely irrelevant to schools out here.

She focused her attention on a point above the speaker's head so it looked like she was listening and let her thoughts wander.

Quinn had been in her thoughts constantly all week. Occasionally, a shaft of fear would spear through her, hoping he hadn't done anything foolish—usually in the early hours when she couldn't get back to sleep and everything seemed so much worse.

One night she'd had a nightmare about him, and it was all she could do not to jump in her car, and drive out to *Merry Downs*.

Her talk with Beth had reassured her a bit.

'Hey Kimmy, what are you doing ringing me at

this time of the morning? I thought you'd be in class by now.'

'Hi, Beth. You never listen to me, do you? I'm not on a class any more. I'm the deputy principal, remember? No kids.'

'I know. I was just teasing,' her sister said, 'but it's still not like you. You're usually immersed in your work at school by now. You're not sick, are you?'

'No, I'm on speakerphone on the way down to Charleville. I've got an in-service for the day and then dinner.'

'Lucky you, I've got a lunch to organise for fifty visiting dignitaries.' Beth was head chef at Parliament House in Brisbane; Kim was proud of the success her sister had made of her career.

'How're things in Augathella?' Beth asked.

'Interesting,' Kim replied slowly.

'Ooh, I like the sound of that. What's interesting in your life, sis?'

'Quinn Calthorpe is back in town.'

'Oh, that's big news. His mum and dad passed away recently, didn't they?'

'Yes, they did and he's living, well sort of living, out at *Merry Downs*.'

'What do you mean "sort of living"?'

'I was worried about him, Beth.' The words spilled from Kim. 'I overheard him say something at the pub the other afternoon. He really worried me.'

'So you were at the pub with him. Quick work.'

'No, listen. I didn't speak to him there. I overheard a conversation. Braden and Callie Cartwright had a lunch there because Petie came home from hospital. Everyone in town just about turned up. The pub was packed.'

'Yes, that's great news. I heard he'd recovered. Jacinta called me the other day. I'm so excited they're moving to Brisbane.'

'Anyway, Jacinta and I were up at the bar, and I noticed Quinn. I was standing close enough that I heard a phone call he had, and I heard a comment that worried me. I think he's depressed.'

'Hang on, go back a step. What does "sort of living" mean? Did you mean he's not with it? Mental health problems?'

'Wait, let me finish. I was worried so after I left school—'

'On a Sunday?' Beth interrupted.

Kim sighed. A conversation with Beth invariably went off on a tangent. 'Stop interrupting me. When I left school, and yes, I was there doing a little bit of work on a Sunday after lunch, I drove out to *Merry Downs* because I was worried, and Bethie, you wouldn't believe it. The place is an absolute dump.'

'A dump? Are you sure you were at the right place?'

'Yes, of course, I was. I spent more time out there than you ever did. But the biggest thing of all was, the homestead's gone. That beautiful house where we had so much fun. It's not there anymore. Only the pool's left, and it's surrounded by long grass and the pump shed's half blown away. It was awful. Just awful.'

'So, where is Quinn living if there's no house?'

'At the old settler's cottage ten kilometres further out. You probably never went there. It's on the way to Paradise Springs. And boy, he was *not* pleased when I turned up.'

'That doesn't sound like Quinn.'

'No, the person I've been talking to is nothing like the Quinn you and I loved.'

'You loved,' Beth said.

'Don't be so literal. You know what I mean.'

'What I do know is that you and he had something special going, but neither of you would ever do anything about it.'

'It wasn't the right time. I wanted to go to uni and he wanted to get away from his mum and dad and go to the Northern Territory.' Kim kept her voice even.

'But I could never understand why you didn't stay in touch.'

'I had my reasons.'

'So what advice do you want me to give you?'

'Do you think I should persevere and push? Do you think I should sit him down and ask him what's wrong? I mean, we haven't been friends for years. I haven't even spoken to him since I saw him on Sunday. Have I got the right to hassle him?'

'Do you still care about him, Kim?'

'Of course I do. We were best friends. He was the best friend I ever had.'

'Well follow your heart. It's not hassling. If you think you need to talk to him, you should.'

'You make it sound so simple.'

'It's not rocket science. If you've got a problem, it's often good to talk it over with someone. If he doesn't want to talk to you, he'll tell you to go away.'

Kim chuckled. 'He's already done that.'

'Oh, did he? And what did you do?'

'I went away,' Kim said. 'After I gave him a piece of my mind.'

'And have you seen him since then?'

'No, I haven't.'

'Okay, I can see why you're reluctant to follow it up, but listen, love, follow your heart. Someone you care for, or you once cared for, is struggling, and maybe there's something you can do to help. Now when are you going to tell me why you pair stopped talking? What happened?'

Kim hesitated. 'It's private. I don't want to talk about it.'

'Kimmy?'

'Yes?'

'Did you ever wonder why you could never settle into a relationship with any of those guys you met at uni? And after uni?'

'Not really.'

'Pull the other one. I'm sure you know it's because you were in love with Quinn Calthorpe. Maybe if you admitted it to yourself, and found the courage to tell him how you felt—or how you feel—it might help him with whatever he's struggling with. It would give him something to focus on.'

Kim didn't reply and there was silence as she mulled over what her sister had said. She had always respected Beth's advice over the years, but this was the first time it had been emotional and personal advice.

'Anyway, love, I've got to run and get my staff in order. I'm running late for work. Give me a call after you talk to him and let me know what's going on. If it's appropriate, say hello from me, too.'

'Will do. Love you, Beth.'

'Love you too.'

##

Eleven years earlier

Kim couldn't take her eyes off the white sandy beach at the base of the cliff, and the crystal-clear water. The warm pools at Paradise Springs were incredibly beautiful, and they lay in the warm water, frolicked, and splashed each other like children for an hour or so.

Quinn had had a strange look on his face for most of the afternoon—ever since she walked in the water after he'd called her a rotten egg. Maybe he thought he'd hurt her feelings, so Kim focused on being extra jovial with him, trying to get a smile back.

They walked out of the water and spread their beach towels on the sand.

'I just can't believe there's white sand out here in the middle of the outback like a little paradise,' Kim said. 'It's a wonder half the town, not to mention tourists, don't come out here.'

'That's why it's called Paradise Springs, doofus. And that's why we always kept it quiet. It's on private property.'

Kim nodded. They had gone through three locked gates to get out here, and Quinn had said there was no road in from the back of the property because of the cliffs.

'But why is it like beach sand?' Kim asked. 'You'd think it would be red dirt, like around all the dams.'

'It's from the erosion of the sandstone cliffs. These are the only hot springs with a beach in the whole district, that I know of, anyway. Maybe there are others and the station owners keep it quiet. We've got a pretty special spot on our place.'

'It is, it's beautiful. Look at that water.' Kim lay back on the towel and stretched out in the late summer sunshine. Uni started next week and from now on, life would change. This would be her last chance to relax. She blinked away the moisture that threatened in her eyes. This would be her last afternoon with Quinn, for who knew how long? She was going to miss him so much.

Kim opened her eyes wide and stared through the lacy fronds of leaves that shaded them from most of the sun. A couple of trees grew up the cliff behind them, creating a shady glade.

'It really is a special place,' she whispered. 'Why haven't we been out here before?'

Quinn was lying on his towel beside her. He rolled over onto his side and propped his chin in his hand and looked down at her. He looked at her for a moment, and she returned his gaze steadily, warmth curling in her stomach. The water from the pool had clumped Quinn's long dark eyelashes together, and she thought what a good-looking man he was becoming.

A man. No longer a boy.

The warm quiver ran lower and goosebumps covered her arms and legs.

Finally, Quinn looked away and sat up. His voice was husky. 'Come on. We'd better eat that cake Mum made for us. It's going to melt if we don't eat it soon. What did you bring?'

'I made some chicken salad bread rolls,' she said.

'Good, show me, wench.'

Kim sat up and shoved his elbow. 'I'm not your wench.'

Quinn looked at her and she couldn't take her eyes off his. Her breath caught when he let out a sharp groan and his hand reached out to touch her face. 'I'm going to miss you so much, Kimmy. I don't even want to go, you know. I'm even thinking I should come to Brisbane and get a job.'

'Really, would you really do that?' she said as excitement coursed through her. Excitement partly from his words, but more from the way Quinn was looking at her.

'I would, but I have no skills and no qualifications suitable for the city. I've got nothing to offer you. Maybe down the track. Give me a couple of years up north. I'll hopefully make my fortune and then we'll see how things go.'

'What do you mean how things go?'

'To see how we feel,' he said.

'I know how I feel,' she said. 'I'm going to miss you big time, Quinn.'

'Only because I'm your mate. You've got your whole uni life ahead of you. You don't want a cow cocky hanging around you in the city.'

'I do, you know. I care for you, Quinn.' Her voice was soft as she reached her hand up to cover his. 'Perhaps we could explore it now, Quinn, before you go away.'

He blinked and then held her eyes again. She wasn't aware of him moving, but before she knew it, Quinn's arms were around her, and his cheek was against hers. Her arms slid up around his back, and his bare skin was warm beneath her fingertips.

'That feels so good,' she said.

'It feels too good,' Quinn said. 'We shouldn't be doing this.'

'Why not? I'm not underage. We're both adults now and we can make our own choices.' Kim tipped her head back slightly.

Quinn slid his lips softly down her cheek until they stopped at the edge of her lips. She turned her head slightly so that her lips met his.

Quinn's lips covered hers and as his arms tightened around her, she let out a happy sigh.

When he lifted his head a few minutes later, he asked, 'Are you sure, Kim?'

'I've never been more sure of anything in my life.'

Chapter 10
Corones Hotel, Charleville
Thursday evening

Craig Wilson stood at a high table at the front of the Corones Hotel deep in conversation with the president of the local branch of the Cattlemen's Association. Braden carried a beer across to him and then headed for the table where Quinn was sitting.

Quinn traced his finger down the condensation on his schooner glass.

'Want to go and sit out in the beer garden?' Braden asked. 'Cooler out there now the sun's gone. I hate air conditioning.'

'Me too, mate. Happy to go outside.' Quinn picked up his beer and followed Braden to the beer garden. There was no one else out there; all the other cattlemen who had been at the meeting were crowded around the bar and at tables in the bistro. Craig and Braden had discussed staying at the pub for dinner.

'Might as well,' Braden said. 'It's going to be late by the time we get home. Suit you, Quinn?'

Quinn nodded, trying to think how much cash he had in his wallet. He'd taken his credit card out the other day. 'Happy to stay. I'm not very hungry.

A bowl of chips and gravy will hit the spot.'

Braden stared at him. 'I'd like to have a bit of a chat. I'm worried about you leaving the property. We've been mates for a bloody long time and I hope you'll take on board what I have to say.'

'Kindergarten, wasn't it?' Quinn prevaricated. He knew Braden was about to ask the hard questions, and he wasn't ready for it.

'Probably. We've known each other all our lives.'

'I'm sorry I lost touch with everyone when I left. I was a bit messed up and the last thing I wanted to do was have contact with the place. It wasn't the same without Kim here. We were best mates.' He hesitated. Why was he talking about Kim when his finances should be on his mind?

Braden raised his eyebrows. 'I always thought you pair would end up together.'

'No. We were friends and I stuffed it up. So I left and I pretty much cut ties. I think Mum was always disappointed she didn't get a Sydney daughter-in-law, but I think she and Dad were happy enough until she got sick.'

'So what's the go with you leaving?'

Quinn nodded. 'Looks like I'll be checking out, mate.'

'What do you mean "checking out"?' Braden asked.

'Vacating the place. Leaving. I'm going to put some feelers out to put the place on the market. Not that I'll get much for it with no fences. Plus, it's so far out of town.'

'Do you really want to?' Braden frowned.

'Oh God, no. Of course, I don't. I only went away to get some space and to learn some new skills. My parents were pretty hard to live with there for a while. Mum trying to marry me off to all the young socialites Dad flew out. In hindsight, maybe I should've stayed. It probably would have saved the place. I'll take on more contract work and get some money saved up, and hopefully one day in the future I can get my own place again around here.

Braden stared at him and his brow furrowed in a deep frown.

'I might be able to give you a hand to get your place going.'

'Win the lottery?' Quinn forced a grin.

'Would you let me put some of my cattle out there?' Braden said. 'It's a waste of pasture to just be sitting there.'

'I'd love to say yes, mate, but there are no fences out there.'

'Leave it with me. If I'm putting my cattle out there, the least I can do is fix the fences.'

Suspicion filtered through Quinn. He knew that Braden had enough of his own pasture and didn't need anywhere to put his cattle. It was a gesture to help him.

'Mate, I appreciate the offer, but it's going to cost a mint.'

'I had my suspicions that something was wrong. Your dad wasn't well and he totally lost interest in the property in the last year or so. He rarely came to town.'

'I should have come home sooner, but it was hard. I was on contract, and we were short of staff. Every time I rang home, Dad assured me the place was going well. Despite the drought, he was keeping on top of it. I got an awful shock when I came back the week before he died. The property looks nothing like the place I grew up.'

'How can we help?' Braden said. 'We can work together and get you going.'

'Braden, you don't have to do that. You don't owe me anything.'

'It's not a matter of owing you anything. It's a matter of looking out for our community. These past weeks have been such an eye-opener for me. We live in a great place, a great community, a great town, a great region, and everyone here will pitch in and give you a hand.'

'I won't take charity.'

'It's not charity,' Braden said.

'It's too late. I've got bills I can't pay. I've got

no income while I'm here. I've got no cattle to sell. And a whole property that needs new fences before any stock can go on. Dad said that last big deluge of rain washed away all the fences on the back block where the grass is lush. If only I had cattle, they'd be fattening up beautifully. I appreciate your offer, but I've got a lot of thinking and a bit of investigating to do. If I could get to the bottom of where the money went, and locate some paperwork, I might have a hope.'

'Let's cut to the chase. I want to help you get out of this mess, and for you to be able to settle down on your family property.'

'Once I get the money back from the aged care home I can clear the debts, but until I find out what happened, and it's a big if, I don't have enough to build a home or stock the place.

'What about putting someone in the house?'

'Word hasn't got round town.'

'What word?' Braden asked his eyebrows raised.

'There is no house anymore.'

'What do you mean? The bank's got it?'

'No, I mean there was no house when I came back from the Territory just before Dad died. I think he was living in the old settlers' cottage down the back when he got sick. The house has gone. All that's left is the chimney.'

'What happened?' Braden's mouth dropped open.

Quinn picked up his beer and took a swig. 'That's the thing. I don't know what happened, and it wasn't claimed on insurance. The old man never said a word.'

'Can you see what's happened?'

'I'd say it burned down, but there's no rubbish left. No roofing iron or anything. Dad lost the plot big time after Mum died so nothing would surprise me.'

'I'm sorry to say that none of us went out and checked on them.'

'Braden, you've had your own issues over the years. I wouldn't have expected you to. I'm his son, I should have come home more often.'

'After Mum died, Dad assured me he was fine. I went back to the Territory and he sounded okay on the phone on our weekly call. It was only when that new doc rang me up and told me that he was in hospital that I came home and found the place in such a state.'

'Have you asked anyone about the house? No one's ever mentioned it, and that sort of news would get around the district pretty quickly.'

'The front gates were padlocked and it looked like no one had been in there for a few weeks. The road was clear of any tracks. I had to get a saw out of my toolbox to get into the place.'

'It's bizarre,' Braden commented.

'It is, but I am going to investigate a bit further. I'd appreciate it if you just keep it all to yourself, I'll do my best to sort out the financial mess and then I'll just have to put the land on the market.'

'Shit, mate, you can't do that.'

'I don't want to,' Quinn said, 'but honestly, Braden, I've got no other choice apart from winning the lottery or coming up with some amazing solution. I'm going to have to.'

Braden looked thoughtful. 'This community has supported me so much over the past few months I'd like to pay it forward.'

'Pay it forward. What do you mean?'

'Put some stock on your back block, fix the fences, and give you a loan to get those cheap steers I was telling you about. It gives you time to investigate.'

'Okay, I'll give—' Quinn was about to agree but Braden's phone buzzed.

'Excuse me a moment mate, I'll take this call. It's Callie. I hope everything is okay.'

Quinn watched as Braden walked across to the other side of the beer garden and frown as he put his hand up to his head and ran his fingers through his short hair. He spoke quietly into his phone for a good five minutes, and when he came back, his expression was full of worry.

Braden shook his head. 'That was Callie. She's in the hospital at Augathella. She's having some problems with her pregnancy so they're sending her down here.'

'That's no good.'

'I'll be staying down here. Callie's called Kim … she's down here and has offered a lift home for you and Craig. She's coming here after dinner.'

'Dinner?'

'She's at the Chinese restaurant at some sort of teacher do.'

'Don't worry about it, mate. You do what you have to. We'll get back to Augathella. How long until Callie's here?'

'They're just putting her in an ambulance now so she'll be an hour or so.'

'What do you want for dinner? You sit down and I'll go and order for you.'

'Thanks, mate. Appreciate it.'

Chapter 11

So, I'll get a chance to have a chat with Kim earlier than I planned, Quinn thought as he sat with Braden while he picked at his meal.

Finally, Braden pushed the plate aside. 'Thanks for getting my dinner. I'll head to the hospital now. They won't be far away.'

'Let us know how Callie is when you get a chance.'

Braden's hand was firm on Quinn's shoulder. 'Thanks, Quinn. It's good to have you back in town.'

Quinn walked to the door with him. 'Hope everything goes well.'

Braden's face was haggard. 'Sometimes I don't know how much more I can take, but I have to stay positive.'

'If there's anything you need, just call,' Quinn said.

'They're sending her down here for a scan as a precaution. Maybe she'll stay in overnight. I can't believe she thought about organising a lift home for you and Craig. She's always so calm. I wonder what she's done with the boys.'

'Where were they?'

'As far as I know, Petie is at Ruth's place. I've

got a number. If I give it to you, can you give her a buzz when you get back to town?'

'Happy to.'

'The other pair were at tennis coaching but I think they were walking home to Ruth's when it finished. Maybe Callie's organised something.' Braden put a hand to his forehead. 'I've got your number; as soon as I see Callie and we sort out what's going on, I'll give you a buzz and let you know. I'm sure she wouldn't have left them at tennis, and anyway, there are heaps of people there to look after them.'

'Braden, calm down. Anyone who organises a lift home for two blokes will have sorted the kids first. I'll chase it up when Kim gets us back to town. If she knows anything when she gets here, I'll let you know.'

'Thanks, mate. Talk later.'

As Braden hurried through the door, Quinn walked back to the table where they'd been sitting. Craig was still over at the bar chatting to somebody else, and Quinn picked idly at his now-cold chips. Thankfully he'd just had enough cash to pay for Braden's meal and his chips, but until he went into the bank tomorrow to arrange some sort of overdraft and early access to his term deposit he was low on cash.

Craig was just walking over to him when the

door opened and Kim walked in. He was able to watch her for a while before she spotted them. She was dressed in a dark grey suit and high heels, and her hair was up on top of her head; he'd never seen her look so elegant.

She spotted them and waved. As she walked over her heels clicked on the tiles. 'Hello, Craig. Hi, Quinn.' She avoided his eyes, and he felt guilty.

'Have you eaten?' she asked looking at the half-empty bowl of chips on the table.

'I'm waiting till I get home,' Craig said. 'I told Braden I was happy to stay but I didn't eat as the missus has got a baked dinner waiting for me.'

'Yes, I've finished mine, thank you, Kim,' Quinn said politely.

'Well, are you right to go?'

Quinn put his hand on her arm, and he froze as a shock tingled his skin, Kim stood still and her eyes met his.

Craig bent down to pick up his briefcase, and Quinn spoke quietly to Kim. 'I want to apologise for Sunday, but we'll talk about that later. Braden was wondering if you knew any more details. You spoke to Callie, didn't you?'

'Yes, she called me. I couldn't believe she was in hospital in Emergency and here she was, calling me to organise a lift for Braden's mates. She's an amazing person; she can handle about ten things at once. Talk about multitasking.'

'Braden spoke to her briefly,' Quinn said, 'but he didn't know what was happening with the two older boys. Did Callie say anything to you?'

'Yes, she did. She said that Pete is at Ruth's, and he's going to stay the night. I'm going to call in and see if they need anything. I might even have to go out to *Kilcoy Station* to pick up some stuff. Ruth's husband, Jeff, was going to walk down to tennis and bring the boys home.'

'Okay, Braden didn't know that. I'll just send him a text, letting him know, because Callie probably isn't at the hospital yet, and he was worried about the boys.' Quinn pulled out his phone and quickly sent a text to Braden.

Boys fine. Will be in touch. Let us know how everything goes.

Craig and Kim were chatting quietly when he put the phone back in his pocket.

'Right. Bad news, guys. I've only got a small hatchback, so you're going to have to toss a coin to see who gets in the front.'

'Quinn's a lot taller than I am,' Craig said. 'He'd never get his legs in the backseat of one of those little cars. I'll take the back.'

They were quiet as they walked out to the street. Kim's car was parked two blocks up towards the main business area, and she clicked the remote as they approached it. It was a small red hatchback, and Quinn could see what she meant. He opened the passenger door, and Craig passed his briefcase to Quinn, curled himself up and managed to climb into the back.

'Thanks, mate.' He pulled the seat back after Quinn passed his briefcase in. Kim went round to the driver-side and opened the door, and Quinn got into the passenger side.

It was a small car, and his knee was close to the gearstick. Once he was settled in, he moved his legs closer to the door, because Kim would be changing gears.

'Unusual to see a manual these days, Kim,' he commented.

'I much prefer manual to automatic,' she said.

'You didn't have your licence when I knew you,' he couldn't help saying. He'd always driven them in the old farm four-wheel drive.

'Well, that was a long time ago,' she said briskly as she started the car. 'You needn't worry, I have it now.'

The tension between them was obvious, despite his apology, and Quinn was aware of Craig hanging off every word.

There was little conversation as they drove out through town, and when they hit the highway, they passed the ambulance heading south.

'I'd say that's Callie now. Braden won't have long to wait.' Kim sighed. 'Oh gosh, I hope she's okay. We had a long chat at school this morning and she's so excited about the baby. She even told me she wasn't going to be working next year because she wants to stay home with the boys and the new bub.'

Quinn couldn't help himself. Kim's hand was on the gearstick. He reached over and patted it gently. 'Be positive. She'll be fine and she's only young. If something does go wrong, they've got plenty of time.'

'Yes, she might be young, but that family's had enough tragedy,' Craig chimed in from the backseat. 'At least the property is going okay and Braden's able to take time off and spend it with the family.'

The car's occupants were silent again for a few kilometres until Craig spoke. 'How are you going across at *Merry Downs,* Quinn?'

'Getting there,' Quinn said.

'I must come out and visit. How many head are you running at the moment?'

'Not a lot.' Quinn tried to think of something to change the subject, but Craig kept talking.

'Your poor dad lost the plot those last few months.'

'Yes, I came home as soon as I knew.'

'I should've gone out to the property when he was in the hospital and kept an eye on it for you, but we didn't even know that he was crook. He had a couple of strange conversations with me before he went to hospital.'

'What sort of conversations?' Quinn asked, wondering if Reg might know something. He thought back to the other day. Reg had said to talk to him if he wanted to. Quinn had dismissed it as Reg's usual gossiping, but maybe it had been his way of saying he knew something.

'He was in the pub in town, sitting with old Reg, and he was talking about the old settler's cottage and how much better it was than the big house. I couldn't believe it because the last time I saw the old place, it was just about derelict.'

'It is,' Quinn said wryly.

'Your dad wasn't very welcoming of visitors those last few months before you came home.'

'I guessed that from the padlocked gates.'

'We should've known something was wrong,' Craig said. 'I'm sorry. I should've been a better neighbour.'

Quinn shook his head. 'Not your responsibility. Craig. I was on the phone with him most days, and I knew something was wrong before he even had the stroke. That's why I came home.'

Quinn glanced across at Kim. Her attention was

focused on the road ahead. Darkness had fallen, and she had the headlights on high beam, obviously keeping a sharp eye out for wildlife.

She must have been aware of him looking because she took her eyes off the road for a second, glancing across at Quinn.

'Are you both needing a lift out to your places?' she asked.

'No, I'm fine, thanks,' Craig said. 'My truck's in the pub car park.'

'Mine's parked down the street from the pub. The car park was full by the time I got there,' Quinn said.

Craig chuckled. 'Reg said he'd keep an eye on mine for me. Not that he needs to, but it makes him feel as though he's got something to do.' He leaned forward. 'Quinn? Did you know Reg and your dad spent a bit of time together in the last few months? They seemed to be pretty good mates. He was sitting with Reg at his table most times I came to town.'

'No, I didn't. But Reg did seem interested in me being back. I'll have a chat with him.'

All was quiet for the remainder of the trip home to Augathella. The small sedan whizzed up the highway and it wasn't long before they passed the sign welcoming visitors to the town.

Kim turned into the pub car park.

'That's mine,' Craig confirmed, pointing to a dusty four-wheel drive beside the gas bottles next to the garbage bins.

She pulled up a couple of carparks away and Quinn opened his door.

'I can walk to mine, Kim. You don't have to drive me.'

'It's okay, I have to go that way.'

Craig came over to the driver's side window. 'Thanks, Kim, really appreciate the lift. See you, Quinn. I'll come over in the next few days. Have a good night.'

Quinn's door was still open.

'Which direction is your car in?' she asked.

Quinn was preoccupied. 'I wonder if Reg is still here.' He glanced at the clock on the dashboard. 'It's after seven.'

'He could be,' Kim said. 'Do you want to go in and see if he is? I have to grab some dinner here; our meeting went over time.'

'I will.' Quinn climbed out and waited while Kim locked the car. He walked around to her and stood close to her. 'I also want to talk to you, Kim.'

'So you didn't get to the Chinese restaurant in Charleville for dinner?' Quinn commented as they crossed the pub car park.

'No, that was the plan, but our meeting went very late.'

'What sort of meeting, was it?'

'The day was supposed to be about student well-being and the updated child protection procedures but when that finished at four o'clock the regional director arrived and he wanted us to look at our planning for next year. School goals, aims and objectives, strategies, all that sort of thing.'

'Sounds, um, interesting.'

Kim sighed. 'My head is full of educational mumbo-jumbo tonight. I know we need to have benchmarks to measure progress, but we waste so much time talking the talk.'

'But you love your job?' Quinn asked. He must have noticed the passion in her voice. She always got carried away when she was talking about education.

'I do. But for now, I'm going to get a takeaway, go home, kick my shoes off and have a wine and try to clear my head. And I'll have to chase up a casual teacher for tomorrow.'

'No sign of Reg. He must've gone home early tonight.'

'If I ate in the pub would you like to join me?' Kim asked. 'You didn't have a proper dinner.'

Chapter 12

Kim had come up with a strategy as she'd sat in the auditorium today, and this would be a good time to begin to put it in place.

Quinn hesitated for a moment. 'If you're happy to have company, I'll join you. We could have that chat.'

'Good,' Kim said.

Since Quinn had apologised to her as soon as he'd seen her, the tension of the week had left her. Her conversation with Beth had given her a plan. She grinned to herself. Strategies, aims, and objectives. She knew the drill.

Kim was going to make sure that Quinn stayed on the station. That way she could keep an eye on him. Whatever he'd planned to do, whatever his "checking out" involved, she was going to make sure he was happy and she'd put a stop to all those negative thoughts. She knew she could help him, and she still cared enough about him to do it.

How much she cared, she wasn't going to think about. Halfway through a boring presentation by the welfare officer this afternoon, Kim had decided to make Quinn Calthorpe fall in love with her. She was going to give him a reason to live, a reason to stay in the region, and a reason to focus on his property.

He didn't need to know that she had a plan for him. She would spend as much time with him as she could. Rekindle their friendship, and then work on making him want to be with her.

Her plan got a bit nebulous after that. She had to think the rest of it through.

'A chat would be good,' she agreed. 'But seeing how Reg has gone, how about we get some takeaway and go back to my place? I think it would be a better place to have a chat. Would that be okay with you?'

'Sounds good, but I'm not hungry,' he said.

'You need to fatten up. Is that too personal a comment?' she said.

'I'm a lean stockman, Kim. I work hard. I eat well and burn it off.' His smile showed he wasn't offended by her observation.

'Good, then I can kick these darn shoes off and slip into something more comfortable.'

Her face heated as she realised what she'd said It almost sounded like a seduction routine.

Bloody heck, step into something more comfortable!

She couldn't help the chuckle that escaped her lips, and he looked at her with a grin.

'What's wrong?'

'Nothing. That just sounded a bit off, didn't it?'

Quinn laughed. 'You had me wondering.'

Kim smiled back. The ice had well and truly broken between them, and even though he still looked gaunt and harried, he was acting more like the Quinn of old.

'Do you know where I live?' she asked. 'Do you remember where Mum and Dad lived?'

'I do.'

'Well, I'm still in their house. Mum and Dad moved to the coast a couple of years after Beth went to university and I came back here when I finished my degree. The place was rented out while I was at uni but Mum and Dad said they were happy for me to move in when I snagged a job at the school here. They hate me paying rent but I insist. They're living in a little house at Redcliffe, and Beth lives at Woody Point, not far from them. She's engaged.'

'I've really lost touch, ' Quinn said. 'I wondered today where all the old crew had got to.'

'I'll fill you in over dinner. Okay now that you know where I am, you go and get your car and drive around and I'll just pick up some takeaway. Are you sure you don't want to eat?'

Quinn hesitated. 'I'll just have some hot chips but I'll pay for them.'

'Don't be silly. I can buy a few chips. I'm just going to grab a hamburger, so I'll order a large serve. Are you sure you don't want a hamburger?'

'No, thank you.'

He wasn't eating properly. No wonder he looked so thin. There was something wrong.

'Would you like a drink while you're waiting for the order?'

'Thank you, that would be good. I'll just have one wine. One of those little bottles of bubbles. Bill knows what I like. I'm a "bubbles" girl these days.'

'I remember you used to be a raspberry Cruiser girl.'

'Oh, God, don't remind me of that. It was the only one I ever drank in my life, and I didn't even finish it. You've got a very good memory, Quinn.'

'I haven't forgotten you, Kim,' he said.

She looked down and spoke softly. 'I haven't forgotten you either, Quinn.'

A good start.

He walked across to the bar while she went to the bistro. Kim glanced across at him, he was so thin. He wasn't just going to have chips, so when Sean came to the counter she ordered two hamburgers with the works and a large chips to go.

'Be about fifteen minutes, Kim,' Sean said.

'Okay, give me a yell when it's ready.'

Quinn was still at the bar, and Kim thought how much things had changed in a few days. He was in the same corner where he'd sat looking miserable on Sunday night. Now, his body language was positive, and she'd seen the occasional grin.

She climbed up onto a stool and reached for the glass that was waiting for her.

'Thank you. You did well,' she said.

'I can't take credit for that. Bill knew what your drink of choice was.'

'You're not drinking?' she asked.

'No, I'm hanging for a cup of tea. I'm hoping you'll give me one at your place.'

'Of course. You shouldn't have bothered with a drink for me.'

'So tell me what you've been doing, Kim?'

'Well, after you left . . .' she looked down. That was the elephant in the room. She didn't want to talk about the night before Quinn left, so she'd brush over it. 'After you left, I headed off to Brisbane and I had four years there doing my education degree. I did honours and that helped me get a job. I was lucky enough to get a job here at home and I've been at the school here ever since. This is the end of my seventh year. I'm the deputy principal and I'm hoping to get the principal's position when he leaves at the end of this term.'

'Wow, you have done well for yourself.' Quinn smiled as though he was proud of what she'd achieved.

'What about you, Quinn? Are you home to stay?'

Kim was surprised by the immediate change in his expression. He didn't speak for a full minute, and when he lifted his head, his eyes were full of anguish.

She couldn't help herself and put a hand out to cover his where it rested on the bar.

'This is why I came out to see you on Sunday, Quinn. I know something is wrong. Do you want to talk about it?'

'I do actually, but not here. Let's talk when we go back to your place.'

His eyes held hers and she found it hard to look away. Her heartbeat picked up and that warmth spread through her again.

For the first time since Quinn Calthorpe had come back to town, Kim admitted to herself that her plan might be motivated by more than the desire to help him.

Chapter 13

Quinn
Eleven years earlier

Every time Kim looked at Quinn or smiled at him, memories washed over him. The memory that had stayed with him most strongly over his years away was one he held closest.

He'd been promising to take Kim out to Paradise Springs for the last eighteen months, and they'd never got there.

So, there was no more fitting place to go for their last afternoon together before he moved away.

Kim had been excited. 'I'll pack a picnic and I'll bring my togs.'

'Sounds good to me.' They planned to spend the whole day out there because it was a forty-five-minute drive from the homestead out to the springs.

She looked at him quizzically. 'Are you sure you've got time to take me out? You're going tomorrow. You don't have to.'

'I want to.'

'I can't believe we're going to be so far apart. Don't you forget to text and ring me.'

'I won't. You're off to uni, heading east and I'm heading north but we will stay in touch.'

'You promise me. I hate the thought of losing

my best mate.' Kim's pretty eyes held his, and the thought of leaving made him ache inside.

'Of course, we will.' Quinn had feelings for Kim, but she was only just eighteen years old to his almost twenty-two. He'd spent the last three years after he left school working with Dad on the station and getting cross with Mum for the procession of events she organised for him to attend. For the RFDS ball in Charleville, she'd organised for some girl from Mungindi to come up. Apparently, her father was a well-known grazier that Mum had met at some do. They'd had nothing in common and barely exchanged a word all night.

Then Mum had got Dad to fly to Sydney and bring back two girls for the Easter ball at Augathella. Mum had been furious when he'd hurt his knee and hadn't gone to the ball. He'd gone to the pub with Kim and a couple of mates instead.

That was the last Easter he'd entered the rodeo. He couldn't risk getting hurt and not being able to work. Quinn was saving; he had a plan. He'd had a bad fall, and he still remembered how upset Kim had been, but they were just mates and he knew that she had no romantic feelings towards him.

She considered him a friend and that's what he would be to her; Quinn knew it was time he moved away and stopped having those thoughts about Kimberly Riordan. He wasn't going to stay at home after three years of working with Dad and putting up with Mum.

It was time to spread his wings and save some money, buy his own place, maybe back at Augathella, maybe somewhere else he discovered in his travels. Excitement filled him at the thought of heading off on an adventure, but it was tinged by sadness, knowing that he and Kim would be so far apart. It was no coincidence that he was leaving town the same week as Kim.

He still had his mates here. Braden Cartwright, Kent Mason and more; all good blokes that he would miss.

Maybe when he'd gone away and grown up a bit, Dad would see that his opinions were worth listening to. The number of times they'd come head to head over the property in the last year or two was actually doing Quinn's head in.

When he told Mum he was moving away her lips pursed in that awful tight circle, and for the first time, he noticed her wrinkles. 'It's okay, Mum. I'm just going north for a while, but it's time I left home and supported myself.'

'Quinn?' His mother's voice was cold.

'Yes, Mum.' He'd been about to go out to the shed and he paused in the doorway.

His mother stood in the kitchen. 'I want to talk to you.'

'I thought that's what we were doing.'

'No, I want to talk to you about this trip of yours. I want to ask you some questions.'

'Dad's waiting for me in the shed.'

'It won't take long.'

'What's stuck in your craw, Mum?'

'I wish you wouldn't speak like that. Have some culture, son. Get some manners.'

Quinn rolled his eyes. Whatever he did wasn't good enough for Mum. She'd come from a rich Bellevue Hill family in Sydney and had always looked down on the local community. It had embarrassed him, and he knew she didn't like Kim.

'Quick, Mum, Dad's calling me.'

'I just want to know if that girl is going with you.'

'Which girl?'

'That Riordan girl. I heard she's leaving town. Thelma at the CWA told me she was going. Is she going away with you?'

'No, Mum, not that it's any of your business; Kim is going off to university to do a teaching degree in Brisbane. Darwin's north. I'm going the other way.'

He tensed at her audible sigh of relief. 'I'm so pleased,' she said.

'Are you?' Quinn couldn't keep the bitterness from his voice.

'Yes, she's not the right one for you.'

'There's nothing between us, Mum. Kim is a good friend. She's a mate to me.'

'I don't believe you, son. I see the way you look at her. I've heard the way you talk to her when you're on the phone every night. How often do you ring Braden? You're not talking to him every night. Don't tell me she's just a friend.'

'Well, Mum, you can think what you want but I'm heading off north tomorrow.' He couldn't resist a parting shot. The way his mother treated Kim upset him. 'Who knows what might happen in the future?'

The next day, when Kim had turned up at the house, his mother had been super friendly to her, and Kim widened her eyes as Mum announced, 'I've made a cake for your picnic.'

Kim pulled a face as Vera went into the pantry. 'Quinn, what's going on with her? Is it laced with poison?' she whispered.

'Possibly.' He swallowed the chuckle as Mum reappeared holding a fancy iced cake.

'I'll put it in a container for you. You have a lovely day, won't you, but don't be late, Quinn. Your flight leaves early in the morning. I'm going to go into the airport to see you off too.'

Vera stared at Kim as she spoke as if to reinforce that he was actually leaving.

118

'I hear you're going to university in Brisbane, Kimberley.'

'Yes, that's right, Mrs Calthorpe. I'm going to be a teacher.'

'That's a wonderful profession. I imagine you're moving to Brisbane and you won't come back to Augathella. I heard your parents are moving.'

'Yes they're moving, but I'll come back here. This is home for me. One day, I'm going to be principal of the primary school.'

'Goodness, that's not very ambitious. Do you really want to come back to the *public* school you attended as a child?'

'Yes, I do. I probably won't see you again, but thank you for your hospitality.

Quinn could almost hear the unspoken *not* as Kimberly thanked his mother.

'Come on, Quinn. Take me to these hot pools.'

They chatted all the way out to Paradise Springs and he'd taken great pleasure in watching Kim's expression when she'd seen the springs.

'Oh wow, look at it. Why haven't we been out here before?'

'Because you've been busy studying and I've been working.

'Oh, what a shame that I'm only discovering it now.'

'I suppose it'll give us something special to visit when I come home.'

'When you come home for a visit.'

'What do you mean?'

'You'll never come back here to live will you, Quinn?'

'No one knows what the future will bring.' Quinn resented her assumption that he wouldn't come home.

'Whatever,' she said. 'I just know how much I'm going to miss spending time with you.' She climbed out of his ute and went to the back for her basket.

'We've got a great friendship, haven't we?' Quinn said softly, wishing dearly it could be more, but he had nothing to offer her. But who knew what would happen after two or three years away?

'First one in's a rotten egg,' Kim said, pulling her dress over her head.

Quinn already had his boardies on. He grinned and took off. 'You're the rotten egg.' The warm water closed over him and he swam to the middle of the pool and turned around.

Kim was walking into the water in a yellow bikini—the briefest bikini he'd ever seen.

Chapter 14

Braden paced the waiting room at Charleville Hospital, waiting for the ambulance to arrive.

It seemed to be hours, but when he glanced at his watch, he'd only been waiting fifteen minutes.

He kept going out to the main door and looking around to the side of the hospital where the ambulance bay was, but it remained empty.

What if something had happened in the ambulance on the way down and they had to pull over? Was that why they were late?

In the end, he couldn't handle it any more, and he called Augathella Hospital and asked to speak to Dr Higgins.

'Braden Cartwright here,' he said when the call was switched through to Harry. 'Sorry to bother you, but I was wondering what time the ambulance left Augathella. They're not here yet.' Harry hesitated and Braden waited for him to answer.

'Hang on. I'll just check.'

Braden waited and walked to the door again.

Harry was back quickly. 'They left about forty-five minutes ago, so they should be there in fifteen or so.'

'That's a relief. I was worried that something happened on the way down.'

'Calm down, Braden. I'm sending Callie down to Charleville as a precautionary measure. She was fine when they left. Don't stress. I suspect what the issue is, but I want a scan to confirm it.'

'Is she really okay?

'She's fine. The baby's signs are stable; the heartbeat is strong. We'll have more information after the ultrasound in an hour or two.'

'You don't think she's losing the baby, do you?'

'No. Braden, be patient. Callie was more worried that you weren't home for the boys. She's organised them to stay at Ruth's house. Is there any way I can help?'

'Thanks for that, Harry. Quinn was going to check on them for me when they got back to Augathella. I'll text him now.'

'If there's anything Laura or I can do, just ask. However, if I'm right, I wouldn't be surprised if Callie comes home later tonight, but don't go driving in the dark out on that road, will you?'

'I won't. I'd rather stay in town closer to the hospital. If needs be, we'll find a motel for the night.'

'Just wait and see what the ultrasound finds.'

'I won't take her home anyway. We're too far out of town if there's an emergency. I've had that experience before, waiting for an ambulance to come and it's not a pleasant one.'

'Braden, take a deep breath. You've got to be strong for Callie too. I'll give you a call later tonight; they'll send the results back to me after the scan just in case there's not a doctor on duty there. The ultrasound technician can't come out and tell you. This shortage of staff everywhere makes it a slow process these days. There's no point Callie staying in emergency if she's okay.'

'Okay, thanks, Doc. I appreciate it. Oh, the ambulance has just arrived.' Brayden disconnected and hurried over to the counter.

The nurse on duty at the emergency counter was on the phone and gestured to Braden that she wouldn't be long. Finally, she hung up the phone. 'How can I help you?'

'My name is Braden Cartwright and my wife is in the ambulance that's just arrived from Augathella. I was hoping to be able to go in and see her.'

'Okay, Mr Cartwright, just give me a couple of minutes and I'll see what's happening. Please take a seat.'

Braden sat in the emergency waiting area. A mother was sitting there, nursing a small baby, and tension gripped his stomach as he looked at the baby sleeping peacefully.

Please don't let anything go wrong. Please let Callie have our baby.

A couple of small children were at the other end of the room playing with cars on the floor. Their happy laughter soothed his nerves a little.

How much time had he spent in hospitals in the last few weeks? Maybe they wouldn't have to stay here long tonight, but that was jumping the gun.

The door opened, and the nurse stood there, gesturing to him. 'Mr Cartwright, you can come through now.'

He jumped up, sent a sympathetic smile to the mother holding the bub and hurried across the lino floor.

'Mrs Cartwright is in the last cubicle at the far end.'

Braden hurried past half a dozen cubicles. The curtains were closed on most; one was open and an elderly man was asleep hooked up to a beeping machine.

He hesitated as he got to the last cubicle; he could hear voices in there. 'Hello?'

'Braden.' Callie's voice came from inside, and the curtain opened; a nurse was in there with her.

Braden hurried over, leaned down and kissed Callie. 'Oh sweetheart, I've been so worried. Are you all right now?'

'We are fine.' Callie's voice trembled, but she smiled. 'I knew I'd go to pieces when I saw you. I love saying that *we're* fine and we are. Harry doesn't seem to think there's anything too much to worry about.'

'I know. I spoke to him. I wonder how long you'll have to wait.'

The nurse stepped into the cubicle. 'We've called the technician in and he'll be here shortly. If you need anything, press your call button. I won't be far away.'

'Thank you. Sit down, Braden. You look exhausted.'

'I'm fine now I'm here with you. Now tell me exactly what happened.'

'Ruth called to say that she'd taken Nigel and Rory to tennis so I decided to stay back while I could and do a little bit of cleaning up. The kids had done painting this afternoon and the classroom was in a mess. I reached up to put something on the top shelf and it was like a cramp in my right side. I thought I'd pulled a muscle, but the pain got really bad. Claudia, a casual teacher, came in and she could see there was something wrong. I was scared when I saw I'd had a little bit of bleeding.'

Braden shook his head. 'I'm sorry I wasn't with you.'

'Claudia was wonderful. She made me sit down and she called the hospital. Harry said to bring me around and she took me there in her car. She waited with me the whole time until I was in the

125

ambulance. I've got a whole new opinion of her.'

'She's the one that you and Kim think is a bit of a ditz.'

'We thought she was, but I think it's a bit of a front that she puts on. She looked after me so well this afternoon.'

'That's good to hear now. You know what this means?' Braden said.

'What?' Callie's eyes narrowed.

'It means you're not going to work anymore.'

She put her hand out and gestured to the chair beside the bed.

'Sit down on that chair and stop towering over me while you tell me what I'm going to do.'

'Calm down, Cal. It's not good to get upset.'

'We'll wait and see what happens, and what the scan says and what the doctor advises. I would like to finish the school year. It's only two days a week for another three weeks. I'd like to finish with my class, but I *will* take the doctor's advice and if they say I should stay home, then I'll stay home.'

Braden ran a hand over his hair. 'It worries me. You being pregnant and we're so far from town. What if something happens? It takes so long to get to town, or if you're home by yourself, or if only you and the boys are there, what would happen? I think we should look at getting a house in town.'

'Braden, stop it! We'll wait and see what

happens. How many women do you know in this district that have had a tribe of kids out on the properties? They come to town and have their babies safely.'

Braden looked down. 'Yes, I know. I just don't want anything else to go wrong.'

Callie reached for his hand. 'Sweetheart, I know you've had a tragedy, but we have to look forward. You can't let the past direct all our actions. We'll wait and see, okay?'

'Okay.' Braden stood and leaned over and kissed her again. 'I love you, Callie Cartwright.'

'And I love you.'

A couple of minutes later, a nurse appeared at the open end of the curtain with a young man in blue scrubs.

'Chocolate,' the man said.

Callie and Braden looked at each other and frowned.

'Chocolate?' Callie said.

'This is the fifth night in a row I've been called in for an ultrasound. I was just about to head to the pub and have dinner. I love when my patients give me chocolate.'

'Well, I'm glad you're in town to be called in,' Braden said. 'I know we have so many locums fly in from Brisbane. I'm happy to shout you a chocolate.'

'I'm pleased too. Are you ready to come up, Mrs Cartwright?'

He shot a cheeky grin Braden's way as they wheeled Callie out. 'Dark chocolate, peppermint. We'll have this young lady back in a while.' He turned back to Callie. 'Have you been drinking the water they gave you?

Callie nodded. 'I have and I'm busting.'

'Good, we won't be long then.'

Braden sat in the chair and put his head back, wondering what else could go wrong.

Chapter 15

Braden's phone buzzed in his pocket just as the door to Emergency opened and the wardsman brought Callie back in.

She smiled at him and went to speak as Braden glanced down at his phone and saw it was Harry Higgins.

'Hang on a minute, love. It's Dr Higgins. Are you okay?'

She nodded and pointed to his phone. 'Take the call.'

He put the phone up to his ear. 'Harry, sorry I put you on hold. Callie just came back in.'

'Not a problem. I have good news for you. Can you put your phone on speaker and then I can talk to you both at the same time?'

'Sure.' He pressed the speaker button. 'Dr Harry wants to talk to us both and he said it's good news.'

A smile wreathed Callie's face and she put a hand on her chest. 'Oh, what a relief.'

'We're on speaker now, Harry.' Braden said, reaching for Callie's hand.

'Hi, Callie. How are you feeling?' Harry's voice boomed over the speakerphone.

Braden switched the volume down a little bit.

'I'm good, Harry. No more pain. No more bleeding.'

'That's good news.'

'So what was it?' Callie asked. 'What did you think it was, Harry?'

'Now take a deep breath. You're fine and the baby's fine, but we do have a problem.'

Callie's eyes widened and she gripped Braden's hand.

'It's not a hundred percent good news, but it's not bad news if that makes sense.'

Callie and Braden looked at each other and Braden shook his head.

'Can you elaborate, please, Harry?'

'Callie, you have a problem with the placenta. It's called placenta previa. Have you heard of that?'

'No, I haven't,' Callie said. 'What does it mean?'

'And what effect will it have on the baby?' Braden asked.

'The placenta is the organ that develops in the uterus during pregnancy and it provides oxygen and nutrients to a growing baby. It also removes waste products from the baby's blood. It attaches to the wall of the uterus, and the baby's umbilical cord arises from it. In simple terms, placenta previa means that the placenta is not across the top of your tummy where it should be.'

'Did you know that, Braden?' Callie looked at Braden. 'I mean what a placenta does.'

Braden nodded. 'I do. Cattle can have around a hundred placentas. Different to humans.'

Callie shook her head. 'I forgot about you and your cattle.'

'Good to hear you both a bit more chirpy now,' Harry said.

'So what does it mean for me, Harry,' Callie asked.

'The good news is that the placenta isn't low. It's not completely covering your cervix, which is what we worry about. If that was the case we would have to do a Caesarean because the placenta can block your cervix and make it impossible for the baby to be born naturally. However, yours is more to the side and we'll watch it as your pregnancy progresses. A monthly ultrasound to keep an eye on it.'

'Oh that is good news,' Callie said.

'The placenta arm may possibly move away from your cervix and it's not too close to it for now so I'm pretty hopeful you can still have a natural birth, but it's good that we've got this early indication because it means you're going to have to be a bit more careful. I'd like you to come in and see me at the hospital when you get home to see how to manage your pregnancy.'

'Manage?' Braden asked.

'No heavy lifting,' Harry replied. 'Anything

over twenty kilograms is out. No standing for long periods. Lots of rest is good. We'll talk about the sex side of things when you come in to see me.'

'Thanks, Harry, that sounds good,' Callie said. 'I've got lots of questions for you. When can Braden and I come in and see you?'

'Well, you can leave Emergency now. Just keep in mind what I said about lifting and too much standing; the sooner I see you, the better. I'll have a look. Give me a minute.' He was back almost immediately. 'Can you come in after school tomorrow?'

Braden chimed in. 'She's not going to school tomorrow. I think work might have to finish early.'

Callie glared at him. 'We'll talk about that when we get home, Braden. Thank you, Harry. We'll see you tomorrow sometime.'

'Okay, see you guys soon. Take care. I'm happy it's nothing we can't manage. You get a good night's sleep, Callie.'

'I will.'

The nurse came to the curtain and said, 'You're right to go whenever you want to, Mrs Cartwright.'

Braden put his hand out as Callie sat up and slid her legs over the side of the bed.

'Could we have a wheelchair to take her out to the car?'

'Braden!' Callie shook her head.

132

'Not a bad idea, Mr Cartwright.' The nurse winked at him

Before Callie could object, Braden leaned down and kissed her.

'Bear with me, Cal. I love you.'

Chapter 16

The last person Kim expected to be in her house tonight was Quinn.

And it was particularly wonderful that it was the Quinn Calthorpe she'd had as a friend all those years ago, who was waiting out in the kitchen for her while she got changed.

She told him to start his hamburger before she went to her room and he'd growled at her teasingly.

'I told you I didn't need anything to eat.'

'You need feeding up, Quinn,' she said. 'I'll just get changed. I'll be back in five.' She stood in the bedroom with the wardrobe door open, wondering what to put on.

If she'd been home alone, she would've pulled on a pair of daggy shorts and an old T-shirt, but with Quinn here, she felt the need to look—not professional, not attractive, but tidy.

But then, if she was going to put her plan into place, she needed to make an effort. Kim scrabbled around in the wardrobe until she found a nice knee-length dress, a sundress with bright yellow and white stripes. The same colour as the bikini she'd worn that last day together. A shaft of regret lodged in her chest as she thought back to that afternoon.

The regret was soon replaced by nerves. She

stood in front of the bathroom mirror, pinched her cheeks, let her hair out, fluffed it up over her shoulders, and took a deep breath before she walked back into the living room.

Quinn sat in the sofa chair with his head back; his eyes were closed. Kim stood quietly in the doorway for a couple of minutes, watching him rest. His eyes had dark shadows beneath them, and he looked exhausted. She went into the kitchen and when she came back out, carrying their meals, Quinn's eyes were open.

He raised his eyebrows when she came out with two plates, each one holding a hamburger and chips.

'I've already eaten. I owe you now.'

'No, you don't. This is my treat and you look like you need fattening up. You're too skinny.'

The Quinn of old grinned widely. 'I'll have you know that I'm a lean, mean stockman. I eat enough and I spend all day out on horseback mustering, and burning up energy. That's made me thin and strong.'

She pulled a face at him. 'Well, I think, you need fattening up, so eat your dinner.' Her smile was sweet and teasing.

Kim relaxed. The banter between them came naturally; it really was like having the old Quinn back.

'I really want to apologise for being so rude to

you the other day,' he said between mouthfuls.

Kim noted that he was wolfing down the burger as though he was starving. She frowned again, wondering what was going on. 'I probably should apologise for going out there and telling you I was worried about you.'

'It's nice to have someone worrying about me. Haven't had that for a long time. It was pretty lonely up in the Territory. Then losing Mum and Dad so close was tough.'

Kim put her hamburger down on the plate. 'May I ask what happened out on the property? I got such a shock when I saw the house was gone.'

'Yes, you may. I'll tell you all about it over a cuppa. Hint, hint.' His eyes crinkled and her heart melted.

'A tea bag or in a pot?'

'A pot of course. I love a woman who makes a pot of tea.'

'Mum taught me well.'

'How are your parents these days?'

'They are. Dad spends his days fishing on Moreton Bay. Mum's joined a heap of organisations, and they're busier than they were before they retired.'

'And you've got the house now.'

'I live here. It's still Mum and Dad's. Oh, and while I think of it, I was talking to Beth earlier and she said to say hello.'

'Lovely Beth. I haven't thought of the guys from school for a long time.'

'She left uni early and trained as a chef, and she's in charge of the kitchens at Parliament House in Brisbane.'

'Wow, she certainly has done well for herself. And what about you, Kim? You said you're happy here and you want to be principal.'

'I am. Augathella is where my heart is, and I think I'll probably spend the rest of my life here.'

He hesitated for a moment, and she paused as she was about to put a chip in her mouth. 'What's wrong?'

'Do you mind if I ask if there's a guy on the scene? Is that why you want to stay here?'

She put the chip in her mouth and chewed slowly, and then shook her head. 'No, just me and my career, and my lovely friends. Did you hear that Sophie and Kent got married a couple of weeks back?'

'Yeah, I heard that from Reg. He filled me in on the happenings and the romances in town.'

'Anyway, enough about me, we're here to talk about you. I'll go and make that pot of tea. White with two?'

'You've got a good memory, Kim.'

A few minutes later, she carried a tray with the

teapot, cups, milk, and sugar out to the living room. She was pleased to see Quinn's plate was clean.

'Thank you. I really enjoyed that burger,' he said as she poured his tea and passed it over.

She raised her eyebrows. 'Tell me what happened out at the property.'

Quinn put his teacup down and looked at his hands on the table in front of him.

'There's a lot more that I don't know than just what happened to the house,' he said. 'When you heard me on the phone the other day—'

'I'm sorry. I really wasn't eavesdropping. I couldn't help overhearing and the way you looked really worried me.'

'I appreciate it. Like I said it's been a long time. The problem is the property is going to rack and ruin and there's no money There's no house. I don't know what happened to Dad's plane. There's very little in the bank, and what's there is tied up in probate. I can't find any of the deeds or any of the insurance papers.'

'So, what does that mean for you, Quinn?' she asked, concern filling her.

'It means that until I can find out what's happened to the house and whether it's covered by insurance, I have no assets. Until I can find the insurance policy and what's happened to all Dad's money, I can't consider keeping *Merry Downs*.'

'What! You can't let it go. That would be awful.' The thought that Quinn was even considering that upset her. No wonder he looked so dreadful.

'You had an accountant for the place, didn't you?'

'Yeah, and that's half the problem. We had the accountant in Charleville when I was home. I used to go down with Dad as I got older, to see how the finances worked. I enjoyed that part of the station work, and I was good at it, and Dad let me take a lot of it over before I left. So I know how much money there should be, but Dad changed to a new accountant in Brisbane. The problem is I can't get onto him and I'm starting to feel as though there's something shonky going on there.'

'Certainly sounds that way if you can't get onto him. What are you doing about it?'

'Well, I was getting my accountant in Darwin to try and chase it up, but he's hard to get onto as well and he's snowed under at the moment.'

Kim reached for her tea cup. 'Have you heard about our new accountant in town? Matt Randall.'

'Yeah, someone mentioned he was the one who saved Petie.'

'He's a great guy. I don't know if you remember Bec Hunter. She grew up here too. I'm not sure how old she is. Anyway, Bec and Matt are together now.

He's moved into her place and he started up his own business and a lot of the graziers are switching to him. I've heard some good feedback already, and it's only been a couple of weeks. He's working hard apparently. Do you reckon it might be worth talking to him and seeing what he can find out?'

Quinn shrugged. 'It's worth a try.'

'It's only early. If you want to get moving on it tonight I can give Bec a call and get them to call over.'

'You've always been a mover, haven't you, Kim?

'You know what you want, and you go for it. And what I want at the moment is for you to be happy, to help solve your problems and stop talking about checking out.' She stared at Quinn and he shook his head.

'Did you really think that's what I meant?'

'I did. And I thought it was so different to the Quinn that I knew because that wasn't you. You were always so happy, the life and soul of the party. Then I saw this guy sitting in the pub, looking thin and haggard and worried, and then I heard you say that, and I panicked. That's why I came tearing out to your place on Sunday night. I wanted to help you.'

Quinn reached out across the table and took her hand.

Kim ignored the jolt that hit her nervous system as his fingers held hers.

'Do you know how nice it is to have a friend back in my life?' he said.

'We were good mates, weren't we?'

Quinn nodded. 'And it would give me the greatest pleasure if we were friends again.'

'Well, you know what friends are for, and if we're going to be friends, I'm really hoping that you're going to be staying, and if that's the case, we need to get moving on this mystery.'

Quinn smiled and held her eyes. 'How about you ring your friend now and see if he'll come around, or we can meet them somewhere.'

'I can guarantee they'll come here. Matt is a coffee tragic, and I have a coffee machine. I'll call them now.'

Chapter 17

The smell of coffee tickled Quinn's nostrils as he sat in the living room of Kim's house with Matt Randall. He didn't know how anyone could drink the stuff, but Matt had a huge mug in front of him.

His partner, Bec, was in the kitchen with Kim.

'Thanks for coming over, Matt, he said. 'Short notice, I know.'

'It's the way of this town,' Matt said. 'The women are the movers and shakers and they've got us working. You wouldn't believe the number of graziers who've contacted me in the last couple of weeks due to word-of-mouth around town.'

'I wish you'd been here a year ago. And you're right, it's a good place to settle. Where did you come from?'

'I grew up at Mareeba on a coffee plantation.' He held up his mug. 'Thus the addiction. I've worked in Cairns since I left school and went to uni. I've had two or three years on the road drifting around singing and playing my guitar. I had a bit of an upset in my life and that's how I ended up in Augathella with my lovely Bec. Love at first sight at the Tambo pub.'

'And it sounds like a whole new career starting,' Quinn said.

'It is. So, from what you said on the phone it's

more a bit of an investigation that we need to do to start with. It's right up my alley. I majored in forensic accountancy at uni.'

'I've never heard of it,' Quinn said.

'Forensic accountants act as financial detectives, examining questionable financial data, investigating fraud, and aiding in civil and criminal investigations. It's an interesting field, and a satisfying one.'

'Mate, if you can find out what happened and find any of the money that belongs to the station, you'll have one very satisfied client who will take you on to look after the place.' Quinn's shoulder sagged as the truth hit home. 'But I really don't hold out much hope. Who knows what Dad did with the money?' He'd given the outline of his circumstances to Matt when Kim had made the call earlier. 'Dad wasn't in a good place mentally, so who knows? I could be wrong suspecting this Brisbane guy. Dad could've given it all away to charity, he could've done anything with it. I'd just like to find out where it's gone. And the other thing I'd like to find out is where all the paperwork is. Whether it got burnt with the house or whether he had it secured somewhere. Paperwork like insurance papers and financial statements, as well as cattle records. He used to be a stickler for record keeping. I can't imagine him getting rid of it. If I can find out what happened to the house, I can claim it on insurance—if there was a current policy—and start building a new one gradually.'

***

Quinn parked his car at the back of the pub. It had been a late night, and by the time Matt and Bec had left, Kim had insisted he stayed the night in the guest room.

'It makes sense; you want to go and see Reg tomorrow, so it would mean a trip out to *Merry Downs* for nothing.'

'Bluey should be okay. I left out plenty of food and water.'

Kim had left for school by the time he woke up, and he went into the kitchen and smiled when he saw she'd left the teapot out, and some sliced bread next to the toaster.

Last night had been great. They'd re-established their friendship, and although the elephant in the room had been there, there was no mention made of their last time together.

After tea and toast, he took a quick shower and headed out. He locked the car and walked towards the pub. He needed to forget that afternoon. They'd been kids and it wasn't a big deal and he needed to let it go.

After he talked to Reg, he was going to head out to the station and have a better look around. See if he could find a place where Dad might have stashed the fire-proof safe. It would have survived the fire. Dad had kept Mum's jewellery in there and his personal papers, so he'd have a good scout around the property and see if he could find it.

Reg was in his usual spot at the door. 'How are you going, young lad?'

'I'm getting there, mate.'

Reg gestured to the empty chair next to him. 'Pull up a pew.'

Quinn was pleased that Reg was receptive to talking to him, but then again, the chance of someone buying him a beer was enough motivation to have a yarn. 'Can we have a bit of a chat?' he asked.

'Always, mate. I've been waiting for you to come back.' Reg screwed his face up as he looked up at him. The morning sun was bright on this side of the building

'A quick one. I'm meeting Matt Randall in a few minutes. If we need more time, I can come back.'

'Nuh, sit down. Won't take long to tell you a few things. Good to see you meeting the new blood in town. I like that young fella.'

'Can I buy you a beer?'

'Thought you'd never offer, mate.'

'Middy or schooner?'

'Do I look like a pansy? Schooner, of course.'

Quinn had a quick look around the pub as he headed to the bar; there was no sign of Matt yet, so he bought Reg a schooner and a Coke for himself. He took the drinks outside.

'None for you?'

'Bit early for me, plus I'm driving out to the station soon.'

'What are you doing out there?'

'Having a bit of a poke around.'

'Your father told me why he did it, you know.'

Quinn's head flew up. 'Did what?'

'Got rid of the house. Bloody shame, I told him, but he wouldn't budge.'

'He did do it?'

'Yep, burnt the lot. Said he watched it burn and it made him feel better. He didn't tell anyone else, and I ain't told a soul. I didn't know if there'd be trouble. Is a man allowed to burn down his own house or is it a crime?'

Quinn found it hard to speak. 'Why did it make him feel better? Why did he do it?'

Reg picked up his beer, took a deep drink and wiped the back of his hand across his mouth. 'Poor bugger said he couldn't stand to look at the house and know Vera wasn't in there. I don't think he was thinking real straight back then.'

'But he told you? And no one else?'

'As far as I know. That's why I keep meself sharp, sitting out here talking to people. I know what's going on and I know when to keep quiet. You'd be surprised what I know, mate. Did you ever hear about—'

'Hang on. I want to know more.'

Reg shrugged. 'Like what?'

'Like where did it go? There's nothing left there.'

'He told me that he got the D4 from down the back of the property.'

'What D4?'

'He had a couple of dozers in a shed right at your back gate.'

'What back gate?' Quinn shook his head. 'There's no back gate to the property.'

'Apparently, there is now. And a couple of sheds. Said he put it all on a truck and dumped it in the gully behind the old house. You need to have a better look, son.'

'Okay, I'm on my way now.' Quinn picked up his glass and stood. 'One more thing. What about his Cessna?'

'Ah, now you're getting there. He sold that to that shonky bastard who used to meet him here at the pub. Wouldn't trust that one.'

'Tell me about him.'

Reg tapped the side of his nose. 'He turned up

to ask your Dad about selling the plane. Right out of the blue, he didn't even have it for sale. He talked your old man into investing with him. Took the plane and said he'd invest what he paid for it. Plus your dad never said, but I'm pretty sure he invested more of his money with him too. He was getting a bit confused by then, and he agreed. Bloody Alzheimers. He talked it over with me a few times over a beer. I told him to be careful, but I was pretty sure there was something dodgy about the whole thing.'

Quinn could barely get his head around it all. 'Reg, I owe you big time. Did Dad tell you anything else?'

'Nuh, that covers it all. Now you stop moping around and feeling sorry for yourself.'

'I'll see you soon, mate. And thank you.' As he left the pub, Quinn detoured via the bar, pulled out his last twenty-dollar note and put it on the counter. 'Another schooner for Reg, and give him some lunch with my compliments, please, mate.'

As he hurried out to the car park, Matt was walking towards the pub.

'Sorry I'm late, Quinn. I've been on the phone all morning. Got a lot to tell you.'

'Matt, I've got news too. I've had a breakthrough. You'll never guess what happened. Have you got time to come out to the station with me?'

'I'm my own boss. I've got all day.'

'Jump in my car and I'll tell you about it on the way out. I have to look for something. Reg told me where the house stuff was dumped and I'm hoping Dad's safe will be there.'

'And I've tracked down your Dad's accounts.'

'Fair dinkum?' Quinn's grin was wide. 'What a morning.' He glanced at his watch. 'It's too late to ring Kim and tell her. I'll send her a text and see her tonight.'

Chapter 18

Kim hummed under her breath as she tackled the timetable for next year. Her spirits had lifted; it was hard to believe that last Sunday she'd been worried about Quinn, and then the week had gone downhill when Callie had ended up in the hospital.

But everything was looking so much better, and she was feeling good. Callie had called on the way back from seeing Dr Higgins at the hospital to say that she wouldn't be back for the next three weeks to teach, but would be happy to come in as a volunteer and help with the Christmas events.

Braden had hovered over her like a mother hen, but Callie assured Kim that she and the baby were fine. She was just going to take it a bit easier.

Kim hugged her as she left her office. 'I'm so happy for you, Callie. I was worried sick last night when you were in Charleville.'

'All good. Dr Harry can manage it, although he has made an appointment for me to see the specialist when he flies into Charleville the week after next.'

'A good plan. And Petie's still good?'

'He is and he's looking forward to the kindergarten orientation day next week. Braden and I will both bring him in. Another big week coming up.'

'Well, you make sure you don't overdo it.'

'Don't worry, I won't. I've had my warning.' Callie looked up at Braden. 'I'm listening to Braden, and I'm listening to what my body tells me.'

Kim went back to her desk when they left. She picked up her phone to call Claudia Ricci to see if she was available to take over Callie's days, but the phone buzzed with a message before she had looked at her contacts.

From Quinn. She smiled and her smile grew wider as she read.

Kim! What a morning. Found out heaps about Dad and the house from Reg, and Matt has tracked down the accountant and Dad's accounts. Everything is looking up. Love Quinn.

Love, Quinn! Kim's heartbeat spiked again. It had been doing that ever since Quinn had arrived back in town. It was accompanied by a warmth that ran through her body and tingling in her fingertips.

Love! She shook herself mentally. Just a greeting. It didn't mean anything.

Having Quinn at her house last night, and knowing that he was asleep in the room two doors down from hers had been—

Had been what? She could think of many words: wonderful, frustrating, hopeful, but just plain good was enough.

151

Take it slow, she told herself. They had renewed a friendship, and they were going to be friends.

Quinn's text held hope, but Kim's main hope was that he would be able to stay in the district.

Her heart told her that there was going to be more than friendship involved if he did.

And if he didn't, she would cross that bridge when she came to it.

Maybe she'd even leave Augathella if she had to.

One thing she did know, she wasn't going to let Quinn Calthorpe leave her again.

Chapter 19

Merry Downs

Anticipation filled Quinn as they drove out to the station.

Matt filled him in on what he discovered as they went along. 'He's well known in Brisbane,' he said. He's fleeced a number of elderly people in the outback. He chooses his targets carefully.'

'How did you get onto him?' Quinn asked. The drive out to *Merry Downs* seemed to be taking forever.

'I tracked him through your dad's Cessna. They had records here at the airport with its registration number, so I got on to a mate in Brisbane. He worked with me in my business when I was in Cairns, and he has a bit to do with the Archerfield Airport. He enquired for me and he discovered who bought the plane off your dad.'

'Great detective work, mate!'

'I love this side of the business. I feel as though I'm making a difference when I can help people get their money back. There is so much dishonesty out there. You wouldn't believe how much. So then I started to investigate this bloke and found that he's been up on some charges, but he got out of them. He's a real smooth talker.'

'So what's he done with Dad's money?'

'Well, from what I can see so far, he's started a new bank account for your father, but he's also a signatory to it. That's how he gets into the money. It's all above board as far as the bank knows, because when he does it, the owner of the account approves him as a signatory. It's a very grey area.' Matt shook his head. 'Most of his clients are elderly men, and he's sourced them through plane ownership. I guess he figures anyone who can afford their own plane, has money.

'He'd drawn $100,000 from your Dad's account before he died, but then of course with his death, probate kicked in.'

'How do you mean?'

'Well it wasn't a joint account, so when someone dies, their bank freezes their accounts where they were the sole account holder, to prevent further transactions and ensure the estate is protected. As it was a sole account and this Darren Goodsir was only a signatory, the account's been frozen.'

'Thank goodness. So, Darren Goodsir. I'd like to meet the bastard.'

'The good news is, he's still under investigation, so we can add your dad's case to it. I've already talked to the investigator, and he was very interested.'

'Mate, you're a legend.'

Matt beamed in the passenger seat. 'Just love my work. It's good to be back into it after bumming around for a couple of years. I owe it to Bec, you know.'

'We owe a lot to our women, I think,' 'Quinn agreed.

'You and Kim?' Matt asked.

'One day, I hope,' Quinn said. 'But I'll take it slowly. Not until I have something to offer her.'

'You will, Quinn.'

'Fingers crossed.'

'Your father's accounts all appeared to have been amalgamated into this one investment account. Goodsir's fleeced a hundred thousand from it, but it's a very healthy six-figure account. And it's frozen until probate is granted. I guess you'll be the beneficiary when that's through?'

Quinn nodded. 'I will.' Lightness filled him and he could feel all his tension drifting away.

'I guess, it's not so critical to find dad's safe now that you've located the accounts.'

'It won't hurt.'

##

An hour later, they stood together at the side of a gully about a kilometre from the settler's cottage, looking down on a tangled mess of roofing iron and various melted objects. Regret lodged in Quinn's throat like a stone and moisture pricked at his eyes as he stared down. If only he'd been home. Maybe he could have stopped Dad, cared for him, and not let him destroy the family home.

'It's only things, mate.' Matt put a hand on his shoulder.

Quinn cleared his throat. 'Yep, but still hard to see the home you grew up in down there in a mess.'

'Come on, we'll go down and have a poke around. See what we can find.'

'Thanks, Matt. I owe you.'

'Do you reckon you'll stay around here, and rebuild the station?'

'Bloody oath, mate. I'm here to stay.'

Epilogue

Kim chuckled to herself as she looked down from the stage. The school choir had just finished singing the Christmas medley and the applause was thunderous. What made her smile was the man sitting in the second back row who was clapping as enthusiastically as the rest of the crowd, even though he didn't have a child at the school.

Quinn had been a different person since his father's matters had been settled. Knowing what had happened to the house had upset him, but he'd managed to retrieve some personal possessions from the mess at the bottom of the gully. She'd been out there a few times, and he'd found some sports trophies and taken them back to the cottage.

The investigation into the fraudster who had fleeced his father had escalated, and he'd been arrested and charged. It was going to be a slow process, but Quinn already had plans in place to build a new house.

She turned and followed the choir offstage and stood beside Callie at the bottom of the steps as the children joined their parents.

'Well done, Cal. That last item was fabulous.'

Callie smiled back at her. 'Thank you. There are some lovely voices in that group.' Callie's pregnancy was starting to show, and she was glowing; the report from the obstetrician had been good but she was still being monitored.

'It was a great idea of yours to have the concert on a Saturday morning,' Kim said. 'All the dads were able to come, and they don't have to face a drive in the dark back to the outlying properties.'

'I think the pub's going to be busy for lunch today.' Callie pointed to the door out to the school foyer. 'Did you see even Reg came to the concert? He was sitting with Quinn.'

'No, did he really! He's such a sweetie. He's really taken Quinn under his wing.'

'Are you going to come to the pub for lunch? Braden's booked a big table. Everyone's coming.'

'Oh, I'd love to, but Quinn's asked me to go on a picnic with him. I'll see if he's organised anything.'

Callie nudged her. 'A bit of romance in the air, methinks?'

Kim shook her head. 'No, just really good friends. We've really re-established our friendship.'

'We'll see. I'm off to find Braden and the boys. They'll be on a high.'

'I'll let you know about lunch before we lock up.'

Kim closed the door to the stage and headed out to the foyer. Most of the parents had collected their children, and she checked around to make sure there were no kids left behind. Quinn was standing at the door waiting.

'Won't be long,' she called out.

Bob had already left so Kim checked the doors were all locked and set the alarm. By the time she got out to Quinn, the car park was empty.

'Did you enjoy that? You didn't have to come, you know.'

'I did. It was very entertaining. I loved the last bit when Callie had the choir.'

'They were great. Speaking of Callie, how organised are you for lunch? She's invited us to join them at the pub with a big group.'

Quinn's face fell. 'If you'd rather do that.'

'No, I'm happy to go on a picnic. In fact, I'd probably prefer it. I've had enough crowds these past few weeks. I'm looking forward to the holidays. If you like I can come out to the station and give you a hand. If you want me to, that is.'

Quinn looked a lot happier. 'That'd be great. And I've got all the picnic stuff in the car. Do you want to go home and get changed?'

'Where are we going?'

'It's a surprise. But you'll need your togs.'

'Are we going to the springs?' Curiosity filtered through her words. They hadn't talked about the springs in the four weeks Quinn had been back.

They hadn't talked about their last day together; they'd both avoided it.

'I'm not saying.'

Quinn followed Kim home in his four-wheel drive and waited in the car while she ran in to get her togs and a towel. She kept the same dress on; it was cool and comfortable, and her favourite colour—the same yellow as the bikini she'd worn the last time she'd been to the springs.

They chatted as Quinn drove, and Kim smiled as they turned into the repaired gates of *Merry Downs*. She had a fairly good idea of where they were going. Maybe it was time to talk about why they had lost touch.

From her side, it had been disappointment tempered with a little bit of anger that Quinn had simply not contacted her, after promising he'd stay in touch. After a while, she had wondered if it was because he'd finally got what he wanted that afternoon. The timing was right for him as he was leaving and she could expect no commitment. She'd been stupid and gullible. She came to believe he'd only befriended her for that.

And she'd fallen for it.

For him.

***

Quinn had spent an hour in IGA before the Saturday morning concert, choosing an array of foods for what he hoped would be a very special occasion. He bought a new esky because the one in his vehicle was stained and dusty. After half an hour of shopping, the esky contained a bag of ice, a selection of cold meats and cheese, strawberries and grapes, and two custard tarts that the lady in the deli had persuaded him to buy. He made a quick detour to the pub to buy a bottle of champagne—it was damn good having money again. His bank in Darwin had finally agreed to release his term deposit after a conference call with him.

When he was at the pub, Reg asked him to sit and chat, and when he'd explained he was going to the school Christmas concert, Reg had asked if he could come too.

'Sure, Reg. You can sit with me.'

As they turned into the gate to *Merry Downs*, he glanced across at Kim and saw the smile playing around her lips.

She looked back at him and her smile widened.

'I was right, wasn't I?'

'You're not just beautiful, you're smart too, Kimmy.'

She blushed as he used the name he'd called her when they were in their teens.

'And yes, you got it. We're off to the springs.'

They drove past the old cottage, and Blue ran out wagging his tail, and then stood in the middle of the dirt road as they sailed past.

'Aw, we should have taken him too,' Kim said.

'Nope, today is for you and me,' Quinn replied. He was nervous, and hoped he hadn't been reading Kim the wrong way. She seemed to like being with him, and they'd had many laughs over the past few weeks. She'd come out to the station each weekend and helped him fix up the old cottage, and they'd sat around a fire outside, and reminisced.

But they'd never talked about that day at the springs.

They drove down the narrow track to the cliffs and Kim sighed as the clear water appeared before them. 'It's just as beautiful as I remembered.'

She climbed out and slipped her sandals off, and left them in the car. Quinn's hands were shaking as he turned the motor off.

'I'll just unload the esky, and then I want to talk to you, so don't get in the water yet.'

'I'll just paddle.' She looked at him curiously, and Quinn thought she looked worried.

As he unloaded the picnic supplies and the two camp chairs he had in the back of the Toyota, he kept an eye on Kim.

Her dark hair held an auburn glow in the midday sunlight, and the slight breeze moulded her dress to her slim figure. When he'd set up their lunch site in the shade, she walked back up to him.

'Would you like something to eat or drink, before we chat?'

'No. I'd like to know what we're going to talk about. You've got me nervous.'

'So am I,' he admitted.

'You're not going to go back to the Territory, are you?' she asked.

'Absolutely not. I'm home to stay.'

'So?' Kim looked as nervous as he felt.

Quinn took a step closer and took her hand. 'I want to explain to you why I didn't call you. I think it's been on both of our minds for the last month. I thought this was a good place to do it.'

She nodded and tipped her head back and looked up at him. His heart beat a little faster as he looked into her pretty eyes.

'That afternoon—'

'Was wonderful,' she finished for him.

Hope surged within. 'It was. But I carried so much guilt. I thought I'd taken advantage of you. I mean, I was going away and we were heading in different directions for a long time. I convinced myself I'd done the wrong thing by you, and I decided to cut ties. I cared so much for you, Kim. Leaving you that afternoon was the hardest thing I've ever done.'

'Past tense?' she said.

'No, I still care for you. I never stopped loving

you. Not the whole time I was away.'

Her eyes widened and that faint pink stained her cheeks. She reached out to him and took his other hand. 'And I feel exactly the same way. I'll be honest. I've had a few boyfriends over the years, but they never lasted, because no one ever measured up to you. I've always loved you since that first afternoon when you sat with me around the pool at the homestead. I've never stopped, and it took me a while to realise that was my motivation for wanting to help you when you first came back to town, and I thought you really wanted to "check out"!'

Quinn put his arms around her and his lips took Kim's in a kiss that sealed their love for each other and promised a future together. Her body was soft and pliant as she leaned into him. She moaned softly when he lifted his head and moved away, reaching into his pocket.

'I didn't tell you what I found in Dad's safe because I was hoping to surprise you one day, but I honestly had no hope it would be so soon. Maybe it is too soon?' He held up his great-grandmother's pale blue sapphire ring. 'It wasn't Mum's, but all of the old jewellery, Mum's and the family collection, were all intact in the safe. Every piece survived the fire.' Quinn looked at the woman he loved and the look on her face filled him with confidence, as he dropped to one knee and held the ring out.

'Kimberley Riordan, will you do me the honour of becoming my wife?'

Tears rolled down her face and Kim dropped to her knees in front of Quinn and put her hands on either side of his face. 'Oh, my love, I will.'

The shadows had lengthened before Kim and Quinn partook of the champagne feast and a swim in Paradise Springs.

This is where we leave the eight Augathella Girls, but the good news is there will be a series of short and sweet stories over the next year to keep up with the local folk.

UNTIL THE NEXT STORIES…
Subscribe to my website to keep up with the release of each story.

www.annieseaton.net

Coming in 2023
A series of short and sweet stories about the Augathella crew. Catch up with old friends, and meet some new characters in:
An Augathella Baby
An Augathella Easter
An Augathella Surprise
An Augathella Wedding
An Augathella Winter
An Augathella Ball
An Augathella Spring
An Augathella Christmas

The Augathella Girls series.

Book 1: Outback Roads –The Nanny
Book 2: Outback Sky – The Pilot
Book 3: Outback Escape – The Sister
Book 4: Outback Winds – The Jillaroo
Book 5: Outback Dawn – The Visitor
Book 6: Outback Moonlight – The Rogue
Book 7: Outback Dust – The Drifter
Book 8: Outback Hope – The Farmer

Soon available in two boxed sets.
The Augathella Girls: Volume 1:
https://books2read.com/u/bMNZ18
The Augathella Girls:
Volume 2: COMING SOON

OTHER BOOKS from ANNIE

Whitsunday Dawn
Undara
Osprey Reef
East of Alice

Porter Sisters Series

Kakadu Sunset
Daintree
Diamond Sky
Hidden Valley
Larapinta
Kakadu Dawn (June 2023)

Pentecost Island Series

Pippa
Eliza
Nell
Tamsin
Evie
Cherry
Odessa
Sienna
Tess
Isla
Also available in three boxed sets
Books 1-3
Books 4-6
Books 7-10

The Augathella Girls Series
Outback Roads
Outback Sky
Outback Escape
Outback Wind
Outback Dawn
Outback Moonlight
Outback Dust
Outback Hope

Sunshine Coast Series
Waiting for Ana
The Trouble with Jack
Healing His Heart
Sunshine Coast Boxed Set

The Richards Brothers Series
The Trouble with Paradise
Marry in Haste
Outback Sunrise
Richards Brothers Boxed Set

Bondi Beach Love Series
Beach House
Beach Music
Beach Walk
Beach Dreams
The House on the Hill

Second Chance Bay Series
Her Outback Playboy
Her Outback Protector

Her Outback Haven
Her Outback Paradise
The McDougalls of Second Chance Bay Boxed Set

Love Across Time Series
Come Back to Me
Follow Me
Finding Home
The Threads that Bind
Love Across Time 1-4 Boxed Set

Bindarra Creek
Worth the Wait
Full Circle
Secrets of River Cottage

Four Seasons Short and Sweet
Ten Days in Paradise
Follow the Sun

Others
Deadly Secrets
Adventures in Time
Silver Valley Witch
The Emerald Necklace
Christmas with the Boss
Her Christmas Star
An Aussie Christmas Duo (the two Christmas novellas)
A Clever Christmas
A Bindarra Creek Duo

About the Author

Annie lives in Australia, on the beautiful north coast of New South Wales. She sits in her writing chair and looks out over the tranquil Pacific Ocean.

She writes contemporary romance and loves telling stories that always have a happily ever after. She lives with her very own hero of many years and they share their home with Toby, the naughtiest dog in the universe, and Barney, the ragdoll puss, who hides when the four grandchildren come to visit.

Stay up to date with her latest releases at her website: http://www.annieseaton.net

www.ingramcontent.com/pod-product-compliance
Lightning Source LLC
Chambersburg PA
CBHW020522120726
47904CB00003B/936